K.

STORM

THE SOKOLOV SERIES

The Russian Renaissance
The Collaborator
Temple of Spies
Kremlin Storm

IAN KHARITONOV

KREMLIN STORM

Copyright © 2018 by Ian Kharitonov

All rights reserved. No part of this publication may be reproduced in any form or by any means without the prior written permission of the copyright holder.

Cover design by Hristo Kovatliev.

This book is a work of fiction. Names, characters, places, and incidents either are products of the author's imagination or are used fictitiously. Any resemblance to actual persons, living or dead, or actual events is purely coincidental.

ISBN: 9781980636441

www.iankharitonov.com

To my Mom. I love you so much.

OVERTURE

EXTREME WEATHER WREAKS HAVOC IN EUROPE

LEEDS, England — The British Prime Minister has sent an extra 1,000 soldiers to aid the rescue efforts in northern England. More than 15,000 properties in Yorkshire and Lancashire have been affected by severe flooding. Forecasts predict record rainfall and violent gales to hit the already-damaged area in the coming days. The latest storm battering Britain is the most devastating in 98 years, according to the Met Office. The heavy rain is expected to bring further misery to large parts of the U.K., with train services already facing disruption.

Kelly Allenby, 35, was rescued from the rooftop of her submerged Leeds home by boat.

"It's a nightmare," she said. "We're all a bit shocked, really. I've never seen anything like it. It's as if Mother Nature declared war on us."

Meanwhile, a different kind of freak weather is affecting the Continent. Widespread forest fires continue to burn in southern Europe. A sizzling heat wave gas set in across several European countries, producing exceptionally dry weather. Fires have ravaged approximately 100,000 hectares of land across the Mediterranean region. The blaze is sweeping through large swathes of forest and scrubland, forcing hundreds of residents to be evacuated from Italian towns,

Balkan villages, and Greek islands. Over 150 wildfires are raging in the Spanish province of Murcia alone.

All-time high temperatures in the French and Swiss Alps are threatening the ski season.

Scientists claim that extreme weather could become the new normal. Last week in Israel, golf-ball-sized hail pelted the streets of Tel Aviv after a surprise thunderstorm.

1

In the cloudless morning sky above the Kremlin, a pair of Mi-24 Hind attack helicopters circled like vultures, prepared to strike. The gunships carried abundant firepower in the form of automatic machine guns, 30mm cannons, and 2,400 kilos worth of bombs and missiles. Both crews had standing orders to unleash their deadly load at the earliest hint of an approaching threat.

Not that the menacing choppers were ever likely to encounter any real targets in downtown Moscow. All the roads leading to the Kremlin had been sealed off by police cordons within a five-kilometer radius. BTR armored personnel carriers blocked access to Red Square. From the cockpits of the Hinds, the streets within the Garden Ring looked deserted, devoid of traffic. Hundreds of parked cars had been towed away. Local shops, cafés, and other businesses kept their doors closed, as instructed by the authorities. In the face of the overwhelming police and military presence, the city appeared dead. There wasn't even a single pedestrian in sight. The fearful population had chosen to heed police warnings and stay in their homes. Anyone who ventured outside risked getting beaten up and arrested.

Such excessive security measures had been brought upon by the ceremony taking place in the Kremlin.

The Presidential inauguration.

The motorcade of the President-elect raced down the empty streets—a swarm of twenty motorcycles surrounding the Mercedes-Maybach S600 Pullman limo, led by a black

G500 Guard, with two more G-Class SUVs in tow, sirens blaring. Speeding past the Cathedral of Christ the Savior, the procession swung off Kremlevskaya Embankment toward St. Basil's Cathedral and entered the Kremlin through the Spassky Gate.

At five minutes to eleven, the Mercedes Pullman halted in front of the Grand Kremlin Palace. The rear door opened and Russia's newly-elected President got out of the car.

Saveliy Ignatievich Frolov had won the election by a landslide 86 percent of the popular vote.

Voter fraud had doubled the actual level of his support, but it hardly mattered. Presidential elections in Russia had long become a formality. Victory was assured through a lack of alternatives. With the political landscape mopped up of dissent, and Frolov's rivals acting as extras in a stage show, the Russian people had merely accepted the predetermined result.

The country no longer faced a period of uncertainty. In the last few tumultuous months, President Nikolai Alexandrov had stepped down from office, and then the nation had learned of his untimely death. Frolov had emerged as the likeliest candidate to maintain the status quo between the power-hungry oligarchs and steer Russia clear of looming chaos. He certainly had the experience to appease the different Kremlin factions, having risen through the ranks of the KGB Fifth Chief Directorate (Internal security against artistic, political, and intellectual dissension). Only the break-up of the Soviet Union had prevented him from becoming a full Politburo member. During Alexandrov's term, Saveliy Frolov had held the position of FSB Director, masterminding policies to restore the country's Soviet might.

Now he was about to rule Russia for the next six years.

The general in charge of the Kremlin Regiment greeted him, snapping to attention.

"Comrade President-Elect of the Russian Federation!"

Frolov gave a curt nod in reply, walking past him through the doors of the Grand Kremlin Palace exactly as the historic Kremlin Clock on the Spasskaya Tower chimed eleven sharp.

Despite Frolov's geriatric age, the man brimmed with energy, his physical condition enhanced by injections of Meldonium. His face was still puffy from the recent Botox shots which had smoothed out the deepest creases etching his skin. An Italian-cut suit disguised his pouchy gut, while elevator shoes made him appear taller.

He climbed the fifty-eight steps of the massive Red Staircase which opened into Kremlin's magnificent halls, already filled with expectant guests. The crowd on either side of the red carpet broke into rapturous applause as soon as Frolov entered St. George's Hall. The ovation gave Frolov a narcotic effect of swelling pride.

St. George's white walls, decorated with bas-relief and marble slabs, converged at a height of 17 meters, dwarfing the six gilded chandeliers which illuminated the 60-meter length of the chamber, the largest in the Grand Kremlin Palace.

Hundreds of men and women flanking his path ogled and cheered. Frolov nodded and mouthed thanks without breaking his stride.

Even at a brisk pace, traversing the cavernous St. George's, St. Alexander's, and finally St. Andrew's took Frolov one minute and fifty seconds. He didn't want the walk to end as he reveled in his moment of glory. The ceremony, too, was a televised show for the world to witness.

At the end of the gold-encrusted St. Andrew's Hall, the red carpet reached a raised platform. The Patriarch of the Russian Orthodox Church stood waiting for Frolov next to the rostrum in the center of the platform. The President-elect joined Patriarch Galaktion to take the oath of office.

As he stepped behind the rostrum to face the crowd, Frolov slapped the Constitution with his right palm as if swatting a fly. When he began reciting the oath, his microphone-amplified voice clipped each word. His eyes narrowed into slits. It seemed like he was sending a veiled message to some unknown enemy.

"*I swear in exercising the powers of the President of the Russian Federation to respect and protect the rights and freedoms of man and citizen, to respect and defend the Constitution of the Russian Federation, to protect the sovereignty and independence, security and integrity of the state, to faithfully serve the people.*"

No sooner had President Frolov uttered the last phrase than the anthem of the Russian Federation reverberated around the hall. The anthem of the Soviet Union and the Bolshevik Party.

The anthem of Joseph Stalin.

2

A stand-up cocktail party followed the official ceremony. The waiting staff of security officers served beverages and hors d'oeuvres to the 3,000 guests.

One man stood apart in the crowd. The tall, athletic figure clad in the full uniform of an EMERCOM commander. The man attracted sidelong glances from the VIPs who were nursing their drinks and conversing in boisterous groups. His sculpted body projected masculinity. He'd been born to wear a uniform like the previous generations in his Cossack lineage. Instead of pursuing a purely military career, however, he'd chosen to work for the Russian agency analogous to the American FEMA.

He never took a sip from his champagne flute, not even a drop to moisten his lips. It wasn't a teetotal lifestyle which explained his abstinence from alcohol. Rather, he found no cause for celebration. His piercing azure-blue eyes scanned the surroundings with a sense of detachment.

Major Eugene Sokolov was no stranger to the Grand Kremlin Palace. It was only a few months since he'd attended a secret meeting in St. George's Hall. He'd been awarded the country's highest military decoration for his role in a covert mission deep inside Kazakhstan. Because of the operation's top-secret status, he couldn't even acknowledge his prior visit to the Kremlin, much less wear the medal in public. He took no pride in his black-ops involvement and wished that it had never happened. It was during the Kazakhstan affair that Sokolov had first crossed paths with FSB Director Saveliy Frolov, becoming his personal enemy.

In Russia, things couldn't get much worse than becoming an enemy of the FSB Director—aside from becoming an enemy of the President himself.

Sokolov's presence at the inauguration was an act of defiance. He could have ignored the invitation, but Eugene Sokolov was the kind of man who stared danger in the eye.

"You don't look very jubilant," said Sokolov's friend and boss, Daniil Klimov.

"I feel like we're attending our own funeral."

"A figure of speech, I hope."

"I guess we'll have to wait and see."

If the new President hated anyone more than Sokolov, it had to be Klimov. General Klimov headed EMERCOM, transforming it from a floundering bureaucracy to one of the world's most efficient organizations. In the aftermath of the terrorist attacks in Moscow, he had forced Frolov to step down as FSB Director. Yet the moral victory had done little to stop Frolov's rise to power. There was no doubt that Frolov would now exact revenge against anyone who had opposed him.

"Finding you here is the only good thing about today."

"Somebody has to watch your back." Sokolov grinned. "Besides, I've wanted to get a look at this place ever since I learned an interesting fact from my brother."

"What exactly did Constantine tell you?"

"St. Andrew's Hall is fake."

"Come on. Seriously?"

"It's an imitation."

Klimov eyed the silk moiré-covered walls, stuccoed ceilings, and the splendor of gilded doors and pylons shining in the light given off by ten massive bronze chandeliers.

"You're kidding me."

"What you see here is not the original chamber built under the Czar. Stalin demolished it in the 1930s and converted the space into a Bolshevik conference room. These are just props constructed in 1999. They're as phony as the election results. And so is everyone inside. Just look at all these people," Sokolov said in a hushed tone. "Parliament members, governors, senators, judges, top military brass, celebrities ... I don't get to see them as often in the flesh as you do, but I've seen enough today. They disgust me. Nothing but a bunch of frauds and sycophants."

"And also thieves, murderers, liars, and corrupt crooks," added the general.

"Each of them is spineless, but collectively, they *are* Frolov. He's simply the worst of them all. It's impossible to win. But it doesn't mean that every decent person left in Russia has to give up."

"You're right, of course. We must keep doing our job the best we can. The name of the man in the Kremlin shouldn't make any difference."

The crowd in front of Sokolov and Klimov parted like the Red Sea before Moses.

"Speak of the devil," Sokolov muttered.

President Saveliy Frolov approached them. FSO bodyguards and state TV cameramen were escorting him. Despite the shoe lifts, the President was dwarfed by the two EMERCOM officers, who towered a good five or six inches over him.

"Ah, there you are, General. I'm so glad you could join us today. I might as well use this opportunity to break the news to you. As you know, the government is in need of a shakeup and I'm afraid that there is no place for you in the new cabinet. It's not my choice. It is the will of the people. You showed your true colors when you sided against eighty-six percent of the population. In these challenging times, Russia has called for true patriots. Not political charlatans or traitors like you. Your time is up. I expect you to hand in your resignation tomorrow."

Without another word, the newly-crowned ruler of Russia turned on his heel and marched off with his cohort, leaving a breathless herd of spectators in his wake.

A private banquet in the palatial Red Salon of the Kremlin was being served for the President and a select few of his closest confidants. A thousand other guests from the second tier were already flocking to the adjacent Manege building, where a day-long feast was about to begin.

St. Andrew's Hall was emptying as Daniil Klimov stood there stone-faced.

"That was a quick resolution," he said. "Our new President doesn't waste time or mince words. Well, it was never likely that he wanted us to stay for dinner. At least the circus is over."

"I don't think we're done with it yet," said Sokolov, nudging his friend. "In fact, the show is only about to start."

"What?"

Klimov followed Sokolov's gaze.

A trio of guards was heading their way—dark suits, crew cuts, bulging muscles, and Neanderthal faces.

"Comrades," said the lead security man, addressing Klimov and Sokolov, "you are asked to leave immediately. In case you're unable to do it on your own, we're here to see you out."

Daniil Klimov, minister and general, let out a mirthless laugh.

"This is ridiculous," said Sokolov.

The head goon motioned with his arm and the two of his henchmen stepped forward, showing intent to use force.

A fourth dan kyokushin karate master, Eugene Sokolov could make all three kiss the elaborately-parqueted floor before anybody blinked an eye.

He also knew when *not* to fight. Sometimes it was wiser to accept defeat. Keeping his fury under control, he accompanied a humiliated Klimov on the way out of the hall. As they moved along the red carpet toward the exit, Sokolov handed his champagne flute to a passing waiter.

It was then that he saw her.

Sokolov picked out her silhouette at the other side the hall and froze in disbelief.

She wore a floral-embroidered, long-sleeved Valentino gown. The silk-chiffon dress accentuated her slim figure, the warm undertone of her skin, and her jet-black hair.

One of the guards shoved him in the back, but Sokolov wouldn't budge.

"Hey, move it!"

His mind barely registered the words. Instead, he stood transfixed by the woman who had disappeared from his life forever.

Sokolov called her name.

Their eyes met.

Panic flashed across her delicate Oriental features but she regained her composure in an instant.

But he'd also seen something else in those hazel-brown eyes—recognition. She wasn't scared of him—she feared *for* him. It had to be the reason she was avoiding him. She darted away, trying to vanish in the crowd.

He was losing her—or was he losing his mind? Dizzying déjà vu came over him. A part of him couldn't believe it was really her. There was something eerie about the Kremlin Palace. Months ago, he'd received his medal from the hands of the late Nikolai Alexandrov—or whoever had acted as his exact double because the President had *already* died. And now, could it be a case of mistaken identity? Impossible. He'd never fail to recognize her.

"What's wrong, Gene?" asked Klimov. "You look like you've seen a ghost."

"I may well have."

He shouted her name again, but his voice faded in the surrounding din.

"Asiyah!"

She was gone.

He spun sharply to chase her.

One of the guards blocked his path. Sokolov pushed his outstretched hand away but the security man grabbed his forearm in a vise-like hold.

"Where do you think you're going?" he growled into Sokolov's ear.

Sokolov broke his grip with a rigid *shuto* strike and thrust his open palm into the man's solar plexus. The swiftness of the motion left the other FSO men bewildered as their comrade doubled over for no apparent reason.

Sokolov realized that Asiyah had followed the President into the Red Salon.

He gave the hunched guard, still gasping for breath, a pat on the back.

"Must be the weather. A storm brewing somewhere. Good thing we're leaving early."

3

Those who used to know him called Constantine Sokolov paranoid. Upon closer consideration, his decision to become a ghost made perfect sense. He lived life on his own terms, but life under a tyrannical government required basic precautions. Staying off the grid didn't prove as difficult as it sounded. His political views had already alienated his former friends and colleagues. The social vacuum freed up a lot of spare time which he spent writing a book on Lazar Kaganovich, Stalin's chief henchman. He required no validation to do his job, even if he was blacklisted from working in his profession.

Likewise, he shunned the cesspit known as social media. He could live without the needless online drama and trivial content. More importantly, all Internet traffic in Russia was monitored. People were routinely arrested for posts, comments, and retweets, so he avoided getting his name flagged. He possessed no debit or credit cards, or bank accounts that could be blocked. He lived off his cash savings and a virtual stash of Bloodcoin, a booming new cryptocurrency. His only family was his younger brother Eugene. To keep in touch with him, or anyone else still interested in his person, he used an anonymous messenger service. The encrypted app was popular with jihadis, white supremacists, human rights activists, and other assorted extremists, which suggested that it worked as advertised. Nonetheless, he limited its use to a minimum, mindful of a possible backdoor which FSB hackers could exploit.

Hence, he preferred a face-to-face conversation with the journalist when he received her message.

They arranged a rendezvous near a 19th century rotunda inside the Neskuchny Garden, which belonged to Gorky Park. Constantine hated the vulgar Soviet abomination that was Gorky Park, but the Garden predated it by a good 150 years, having been part of Prince Trubetskoy's estate. It was a site which the historian in him couldn't resist.

He'd met her once before. Magdalena Jankowska was the Moscow correspondent for *Rzeczpospolita*, one of the biggest Polish newspapers. His lectures on the Katyn massacre had made it to the back pages in Poland—or rather, his dismissal caused by his principled stance on the matter. She'd contacted him for comment, and he'd enjoyed their brief chat.

Apparently, so had she, because she wanted to follow up with a full-length interview. Only now the topic turned to the Presidential inauguration.

"*Dzień dobry*! And it *is* a fine day, isn't it?" She spoke with an adorable Polish accent.

They were strolling down a footpath shaded by linden and maple trees which lined the sun-kissed lawns around them. A gentle wind caressed her ash-blonde hair.

"Indeed. And you look stunning in this weather, Magda."

Her beauty appealed to him as much as her wit. A silk blouse, nude heels, and cropped skinny pants combined to show off her sensational figure and perfect legs.

"Thank you." A shy smile. The soft peony-pink lipstick highlighted her pale skin tone. Her aquamarine eyes sparkled behind oversized, geek-chic specs. "You're the nicest Russian man I've talked to ever since I came here."

"You don't know me too well, Madga. I'm not nice at all sometimes. Far from it."

"That's even better." She fluttered her lashes.

He still attracted female attention, thanks to a healthy lifestyle in his twenties and early thirties. He wore nothing flashy—a plain black poplin shirt half-tucked into jeans—

but he looked fit and handsome enough for younger women to start flirting with him. Despite her charms, his interest in Magda Jankowska was purely professional. After his last relationship, he didn't want to get emotionally involved with a woman and make himself vulnerable.

They walked over to an unoccupied bench. As they sat down, Magda took a spiral notebook out of her handbag.

"Are you sure I'm the right person to ask about the inauguration? My brother is every bit as nice, plus he attended the actual event."

Her tone became serious.

"Yes, I know. I do have a copy of the guest list. Thanks for the suggestion, but I'd like to add some historical perspective to my piece. And unless you've changed your mind, it's *your* point of view that interests me. An honest historian is hard to find these days."

"Likewise an honest journalist like yourself. I'm all yours, Magda."

"First of all, what does it feel like to have Saveliy Frolov as the new Czar in the Kremlin?"

"Czar? I'm sorry, but such a metaphor is wide of the mark. Frolov is no royalty. He has the mindset of a small-time hood, and a background to match."

"But hasn't Russia adopted a foreign policy of neo-imperialism?"

"*Neo-Bolshevism* is a better word. It's a policy that's only been around for the last hundred years or so. You see, the Russian Empire had always been an integral part of Europe, not a threat to it. A pillar of Christian civilization. The Russian Czars were no different from other rulers of Europe—in fact, they were tied by blood. The Western monarchies were inter-related, including the Holstein-Gottorp dynasty, better known as the House of Romanov. All of that was thrown out of the window in 1917. Russia went off track as a cultured European country and plunged into the abyss of tyranny and cruelty that was typically Asian, if anything. And Russia has never recovered from this abhorrent state. Frolov is a mere successor of those who started it. A Stalinist, by his own admission. He isn't the Lord's Anointed. He's an Oriental despot."

Constantine glimpsed Madga scribble: *Chan Kremlowski.*

The Kremlin Khan.

Very good, he thought.

"What about Frolov's close relations with the Russian Orthodox Church?" she inquired.

"It's got more to do with business interests than Christianity. Besides, the concept of Orthodox Stalinism originated back in the 1930s. As far as I'm concerned, it's just another ideological ploy."

"Do you see Russia reverting to communism under the new President, then?"

"In some way, yes, but not in the North Korean sense. Frolov can do without it. He's not a Marxist fanatic, either. The Soviets used communism as a tool to control the masses. Nothing more. Frolov doesn't have any fixed political principles. His only aim is to stay in power by any means possible."

"A new Cold War looms. Can the West stand up to resurgent KGB tactics? Will we see the sides face off in a cat-and-mouse spy game?"

"People perceive the Cold War as a geopolitical chess match, played by high-level strategists moving pieces across the global board. This misconception bears no resemblance to reality."

"And what do you think is really going on behind the scenes?"

"It's like trying to play chess against street-corner punks. You can't expect them to play by any rules. They're just waiting to hit you in the face. Only in Frolov's case, the punks got their hands on nuclear weapons."

"You're painting a pretty scary picture."

"It shouldn't look as bleak for the West as it does for Russia, provided the Western countries do not sit idly while

Frolov tests their weaknesses. The Russian economy is crumbling under pressure. Nobody wants to deal with a country run by a hoodlum. World leaders stand united in their opposition to the Kremlin regime. Frolov will never get accepted at the big boys' table unless some sort of discord grows between the U.S. and Europe."

"What strategy would *you* choose if you were in Frolov's shoes?"

Constantine gave the question a few seconds' thought.

"The endgame is to destabilize NATO and break up the EU. First, I would attempt to diminish U.S. influence in Europe. Anything goes. I'd lend underhand support to the most far-out politicians on both sides of the Atlantic. To earn their trust, I'd pose as a progressive socialist with the ultra-left and a staunch traditionalist with the ultra-right. I would try to discredit the U.S. through the media and the Internet. I'd launch cyber-attacks against the Western financial and energy sectors. I'd make use of any crisis to undermine EU security, right down to terrorist attacks. Direct military aggression against a lesser EU or NATO member could discredit both organizations and lead to calls for their dissolution."

"Doesn't sound *too* far-fetched."

"Frolov could be willing to take a wild gamble."

She put her notebook aside. "Off the record, do you think that a similar plan might be developing inside the Kremlin?"

"Without doubt."

"What makes you so sure?"

"I know what such men are capable of, from historical knowledge as well as personal experience."

"So do I," she responded solemnly. "My great-grandfather died in Katyn. I'd hate to see history repeat itself."

"I believe that history is not just a collection of old facts. A nation's history is a way of national self-consciousness. *Historia magistra vita est*—history is life's teacher. Moral philosophy backed up by real evidence. The moral compass of Polish history has put your country on the right track. The Russians will keep on blundering in the dark until they look back on their past in the light of truth."

"Thanks for your time today, Constantine. It's always a pleasure to speak with you. I hope we'll have more interviews in the future."

"Likewise. I'd be delighted if we could meet again for a chat—over dinner, perhaps."

The aquamarine eyes gave him a quizzical look.

"Are you asking me out?"

"Why not?"

"Journalism ethics."

"A poor excuse. Too many gray areas. I fail to see any conflict of interest, anyway."

Magda smiled coyly.

"Well, I guess the line between friendship and romance *is* a bit blurry. *Dobrze!* Let's go out on a date. But I get to choose the time and place, okay?"

"Fine by me."

"How does the day after tomorrow sound?"

"The Fourth of July?"

"Yes. U.S. Independence Day."

"Great. What about the venue?"

"Why, the formal celebration held by the U.S. Embassy, of course. I got a plus-one invitation to the party."

"That's too much history for me to pass up."

4

Saveliy Frolov hated computers, for reasons other than privacy or security. Quite simply, he was technologically impaired. His first day in office began with poring over the printed pages of three intelligence briefs. The room was located on the second floor of the Kremlin Senate. The triangle-shaped edifice with a green dome visible from Red Square had been constructed in 1776–1788 under Catherine the Great. The President's office was located on the second floor of the three-story neoclassical building. Nothing was left of its original decor, ruined by renovation in 1994. Compared to the Oval Office in Washington, DC, it appeared rather drab. No artwork, no history. Beige carpeting covered the floor. The wainscot paneling of the walls matched the solid oak furniture: a conference table, assorted chairs, a couple of tall bookcases, and a desk. A contemporary desk set carved from malachite was the only decoration which caught the eye. The place reminded Frolov of his old office at the KGB Lubyanka headquarters. Just the way he liked it.

A pair of flags behind his desk made all the difference. The Russian flag and the President's flag. Symbols of Frolov's newfound power. Now Frolov had to decide how to best use it.

The first top-secret document had arrived from the Ministry of Finance. The report detailed the plight of the Russian economy. The imposed sanctions had choked it, slowly but surely. The country's Gross Domestic Product had dropped below that of New York City. Cut off from international financing, Russia's major banks and energy companies were facing bankruptcy, so their debts had to be covered by the struggling federal budget. Its foreign-exchange reserves had been drained just to keep the Ruble afloat. Already hit by dropping oil prices, the sluggish economy stood on the brink of collapse. Nothing could save it unless the sanctions were lifted—and soon.

On a personal level, the FBI had tightened the noose around the top Russian officials who had looted their country's wealth—including Frolov himself. A few billion dollars hidden in offshore bank accounts had been seized during a money-laundering probe.

Geopolitical escapades like the Ukraine crisis had come at a price. Military muscle-flexing would only put more strain on the economy, and incur a new round of sanctions that would kill it. The Kremlin had no resources to challenge the West, no allies to turn to, no leverage to negotiate a way out of the financial death spiral.

Rogue countries like North Korea had only one diplomatic tool at their disposal. Nuclear blackmail.

Was it a card worth playing?

Frolov studied the second report, sent by the Defense Ministry. It described the sorry state of the Russian nuclear arsenal. Frolov found the truth hard to swallow. In the event of direct military conflict against NATO, the Kremlin didn't stand a chance. Defeat in the Cold War had effectively spelled the loss of nuclear superpower status. Little remained of the 40,000 Soviet warheads stockpiled at the height of the arms race. Nuclear arms reduction treaties had cut the stockpiles down to 2,500 ICBMs. Most of those missiles had exceeded their service life. All but 232 had an expiry date of 2015. Despite the recent boost in military expenditure, Russia was finding it difficult to put new missiles into service. The nuclear reactors in Ozersk and Seversk, and the Krasnoyarsk-26 plant capable of making weapons-grade plutonium had shut down years ago.

The SS-18 Satan, deemed as a first-strike advantage weapon, had last entered production in 1988. The number of SS-18 missiles still in service had gradually reduced to 46, all due for life extension, which now seemed unlikely. *Yuzhmash*, the company servicing the ICBMs, was based in Ukraine. The guidance systems for SS-19 and SS-25 missiles came from Kharkov, Ukraine. Twenty percent of Russia's uranium ore had also been supplied by the Ukrainian *Zhovti Vody* facility.

The loss of Ukraine had proved extremely costly, going far beyond fiscal damage.

Those Russian ICBMs that weren't obsolete could never penetrate NATO's missile defense shield, which had the capability to intercept each and every one of them at launch. There would be hell to pay in retaliation. A single hypersonic cruise missile fired at the Kremlin from the U.S. Prompt Global Strike system would be enough.

No, a game of nuclear poker was far too dangerous. Even the mighty Soviet Union had acknowledged the risk after the stalemate of the Cuban Missile Crisis. Today, the parity was gone. The Western leaders would call Frolov's bluff. It was no longer a question of assured *mutual* destruction. It was suicide. David and Goliath.

The pressure on the West had to come from within, applied covertly.

Espionage had played a secondary role in Soviet clandestine activities. The KGB's main weapon had always been terrorism. Moscow had inspired every terrorist attack throughout the Cold War, from high-profile political assassinations to plane hijackings and street bombings. The days of Carlos the Jackal and the Baader-Meinhof gang were long gone, but the KGB had amassed a wealth of practical experience supporting such terrorist groups as the PLO or Hezbollah. And creating them.

The third and final brief, courtesy of the Lubyanka, explored the possible outcome of a terrorist strike in the heart of Europe. Frolov smiled as he read it.

The plan was foolproof, leaving no trace of the Kremlin's involvement.

And it had already been set in motion.

A black flag operation—or *green*, rather, flying the colors of Islamic terrorism.

It would work. It always did.

As President, Saveliy Frolov had taken charge of another false flag operation left to him by his predecessors, perhaps the longest-running ruse yet. He swiveled in his chair. The deception was there for everyone to see. So far, it had gone unnoticed even after decades in plain view.

The Red Banner may have been taken down, but it was still the Soviet Empire hiding behind the Russian flag.

5

There would be no fireworks, banned by the Moscow authorities, but otherwise the official celebration at the U.S. Ambassador's Residence felt as festive as any Fourth of July party back in the States. Out in the garden, a couple of hundred guests were enjoying beer, hot dogs, cupcakes, and live country music. American flags, three-colored balloon columns, and lovely summer weather set a relaxed atmosphere.

A northern summer sky was still sun-filled at 7:15 p.m. sharp, when U.S. Marine Guards in blue dress uniform marched to the tune of the Liberty Bell, carrying the national colors and the Marine Corps flag. A moving a cappella rendition of The Star-Spangled Banner ended the ceremony.

Constantine and Magda were standing on the manicured lawn in front the two-story neoclassical building. It was a masterpiece of perfect symmetry and grandeur revived from antiquity. A prominent colonnade and Palladian windows formed the exterior style. On Independence Day, the portico was draped with the Stars and Stripes and decorated with patriotic bunting.

"I love this place. Spaso House is so beautiful," Magda said.

Spaso House was short for the overly difficult address of the residence, located at Number 10, Spasopeskovskaya Square.

"It is," Constantine agreed. "The mansion belonged to

Vtorov, a wealthy banker and industrialist, nicknamed the Russian J.P. Morgan. He commissioned the construction in 1913, shortly before he died."

"What happened to him?"

"Despite pledging allegiance to the Revolution, he was murdered in 1918. The Bolsheviks appropriated his estate from the rightful owners as his family was forced to flee the country."

"How terrible."

"Spaso House has quite a colorful history. The Americans leased it in 1933 when they established diplomatic relations with the Soviet Union. The American diplomats were enamored with the Soviets initially. They held lavish parties for top Bolsheviks, even bringing Moscow Zoo animals into the mansion's living room for entertainment."

"Thankfully, there's no need for such shenanigans today."

"Agreed. Not too many Bolsheviks in sight. In fact, it looks like I'm the only Russian around here," Constantine said, half-joking.

"You might be right, actually," Magda replied. "Most of the guests are foreign journalists and diplomats from other embassies. The relations between the U.S. and Russia have hit rock bottom, especially after the expulsion of 755 American staff. In previous years, up to 3,000 people used to turn up for Independence Day parties, including Russian celebrities and politicians. Nowadays, very few Russians risk showing up here for fear of being labeled as traitors. I hope you don't regret joining me."

"It's been a blast, especially in your company. I guess it's risky to be seen around Russians nowadays as well."

"Great to see everyone having a good time," said a voice behind them. "Personally, I love a good Russian collusion."

The man spoke perfect Russian, with only the barest hint of an American accent. He wore a formal suit, livened up by a Stars-and-Stripes tie, and a genuine smile on his face, which reflected his sense of humor. He was physically fit, but his receding hairline suggested that he was in his forties.

Magda made the introductions. "Stephen, this is Constantine Sokolov."

"Stephen Hilton the Third," said the American. "No relation to the hotel chain."

"And 'the Third'—as in Third Secretary?"

"Not quite." Hilton chuckled. "My father and grandfather were also named Stephen."

"Stephen and I go a long way back," Magda said.

"Yes, we first met during my assignment to Warsaw."

"Constantine is a historian, and he was telling me a few facts about Spaso House."

"Excellent. I'm a huge history buff myself," said Hilton. "Here's an interesting tidbit. In 1946, a group of Soviet school kids presented a wooden replica of the Great Seal of the United States as a gift to Ambassador Harriman. Only six years later, under Ambassador Kennan, did a counter-surveillance team discover a listening device hidden inside it. All that time, it had been hanging right inside the Ambassador's office. The Great Seal Bug is currently on display at the National Cryptologic Museum of the NSA."

"That's fascinating," Magda said, "and almost unbelievable."

"It's true, though. I must admit it's not the proudest moment in Spaso House history. The Soviets had promised not to spy on us, but we should've known better."

Constantine shrugged. "The U.S. should have known better than to recognize the Soviet Union in the first place. *Ex injuria jus non oritur.*"

"Well, that's one way to look at it."

"What does it mean?" Magda asked.

"*Law does not arise from injustice*," Hilton translated. "It's a basic principle of international law."

"The Bolshevik government had been criminal from the start, and no amount of time could change the fact. Illegal acts cannot create law. Not then, not now, not ever."

"In the defense of U.S. diplomacy, I can only say that the Soviet Union is gone."

"I wouldn't be too sure about that. What color is the Kremlin?"

"I beg your pardon?" Hilton frowned.

"Magda?"

She gave Constantine a baffled look. "Why, *red*, of course."

"The Kremlin should be white, as it had originally been until the twentieth century. It was Stalin who had it painted red. Make no mistake, the Soviet legacy isn't gone from this country. And it won't be shaken off anytime soon. Not until the Kremlin is white again, until the red stars are toppled from its spires, and Lenin's rotten, mummified corpse is no longer desecrating Red Square."

"And what would it take to make that happen?"

"A trial against Bolshevism."

Hilton nodded pensively.

"Personally, I agree. A crime is still a crime even one hundred years later. And statutory limitations shouldn't apply to crimes against humanity. Justice is one of America's founding principles. But I imagine that would be highly unlikely in Russia, as things stand."

"The Polish President has called for an international tribunal," Magda said. "Several other Eastern European leaders have joined him. It would be a good start."

"Easy to see why the idea is at the top of their agenda," Hilton said. "The former Warsaw Pact members are striving to protect their independence. Poland, the Baltic states, and Ukraine have formed a buffer belt between Russia and the West. Naturally, they want to overcome Russian influence. Communist history still gives the Kremlin a foothold in Eastern Europe. Security has become a major concern for these countries, so they're taking pre-emptive measures against hybrid warfare. Condemning the Soviet occupation would send a clear message to those who might want to restore it."

"Protecting peace in Europe is way down the priority list for your President, though," Magda noted. "In the event of a real threat from Moscow, it seems that the White House would choose to placate the Kremlin rather than stand up against it."

There was an edge of determination in Hilton's voice. "As any diplomat will tell you, nobody wants to get involved in a new Cold War—or risk a hot one. But believe me when I say that we are taking Russia seriously. We're well aware that President Frolov is planning to throw Europe into turmoil."

"How odd. Just a few days ago, Constantine told me the same thing."

"Really? Confidentially speaking, it's far worse than anything you can imagine."

"Any hints, Stephen?" she clung to his arm. "You know I won't let you go until you tell me."

"Strictly off the record, Magda. I'm serious."

"Of course. I'm asking as a friend, unofficially. Just point me in the right direction. Which trend should I be looking at?"

"All right. Suffice it to say that Frolov is getting rid of any top-ranking official who might oppose his plan. For example, the head of EMERCOM, General Daniil Klimov, has been sacked. His replacement is yet to be announced."

"What does it mean? Does Frolov want to put his own man in charge of EMERCOM?"

"I would hazard a guess that Frolov wants to dissolve EMERCOM altogether. It has become too independent under Klimov, so a major reshuffle would see its functions shared between the Ministry of Defense and the FSB."

Magda turned to Constantine in surprise. "Your brother works for EMERCOM, doesn't he?"

"That's right," Constantine admitted. "Major Eugene Sokolov."

"Is he close to Klimov?" Stephen Hilton III was playing a game of some sort, testing him, gauging his reaction.

Constantine had to tread carefully.

"They're lifelong friends. Does it matter?"

"It could be become a decisive factor. Typically, a disaster is caused by a chain of events leading up to it. Your brother will tell you as much. And at some point, these isolated events combine to make tragedy inevitable."

"Like the assassination of Archduke Franz Ferdinand resulting in the outbreak of the First World War."

"You get the idea. I'm talking about the worst-case scenario here, but Frolov's actions support my theory. A terrorist attack in Western Europe is growing increasingly probable. With each passing day, Frolov is edging closer toward it. Right now, there's maybe a twenty percent chance, but the odds are slashing rapidly. It may become reality in a matter of weeks. A lot of people will die."

"*Boże*," Magda exclaimed. "What makes you think it will happen?"

"Do you know a woman named Asiyah Kasymova?"

A wave of apprehension washed over Constantine.

"Is she related to the late Timur Kasymov?" asked Magda.

"Indeed. She's the daughter of the Kazakhstani President. And recently, she has been sighted in Moscow."

"Why is this important?"

"It's very likely that Asiyah Kasymova is involved in the conspiracy. We have an extensive file on her. Back in Kazakhstan, she underwent training at one of her father's terrorist camps. Langley wanted to win Kasymov over to our side, aiding him with the development of Project Renaissance, an experimental military technology. The Russians were pushing for reunification with Kazakhstan, eyeing another land grab. In the end, the late President Kasymov double-crossed both the White House and the Kremlin. He was killed during the Russian assault on the secret research facility somewhere in Kazakhstan. Asiyah escaped and vanished into thin air. We now know that she had struck a deal with Frolov: her life in exchange for her loyalty. She's spent all this time in Sochi under FSB protection. Now her services have been called upon once again."

"To what end?"

"Apart from her deadly combat skills, she has a professional scientific background. We expect the terrorists to utilize non-conventional weapons."

Career diplomats didn't drop such bombshells. Not even to the most trusted journalists. And not in front of virtual strangers. Constantine was puzzled. realized that the whole charade was meant for him, but why? Then it hit him. *We are taking Russia seriously.* He'd read that the U.S. intelligence community was less than impressed with the White House administration's attitude toward Russia. A splinter group within the CIA was nearing open revolt.

"Non-conventional?" Magda repeated. "Such as the project you mentioned?"

"Thankfully, Project R proved to be a failure, never yielding reliable results beyond the early testing stage. No, what we're dealing with is far more dangerous. It's the single most destructive weapon ever created. Nuclear, biological, and chemical warfare is child's play compared to it."

"You're scaring me, Stephen."

"It's code-named Mercury-18. A program conceived by Soviet scientists shortly before the break-up. The potential of Mercury-18 is unparalleled and truly cataclysmic if unleashed. Millions of lives are at stake."

"Sounds overly dramatic," Constantine said.

"Ask your brother, if you don't trust me."

"I will."

"There's something else you can do. If you want to stop Frolov, let me know anything you might learn about Mercury-18. We cannot allow it to be initiated. And as for Asiyah Kasymova, she's every bit a victim of Frolov's scheme, but she must be found and stopped. One simple step may prevent the disaster sequence from falling into place. You can make a difference."

"I can't make any commitments."

"Listen, Constantine. I know that you've been going through a difficult time. I can help. We'll discuss that later, but rest assured that you'll have my full backing."

"Thanks for your concern."

"I'm not pushing you. Think it over. Your own life can change quickly. It all depends on your decision–or *in*decision. You can get in touch with me through Magdalena."

Constantine said nothing. He'd never imagined it would happen so matter-of-factly. He had just been recruited as a CIA human intelligence asset.

6

Twilight ended at quarter past eleven, and darkness finally reigned over Moscow. Constantine met up with Eugene at a McDonald's a few blocks away from Constantine's apartment. With less than an hour remaining until the place closed, the two of them sat alone under the glow of menu display boards and overhead lighting. Constantine had picked a table to make sure that the employee behind the counter was out of earshot. Eugene had completed a twelve-hour shift of standby duty at the EMERCOM rapid-response facility, so he decimated an entire box of McNuggets. Constantine sipped tepid coffee overpowered by the flavor of the polystyrene cup.

"You should've opted for a Big Mac," Eugene said as he finished his fries and wiped his fingers with a napkin. "It's the Fourth of July, after all."

"And nothing seems more American than the Big Mac, right? Back in 1990 when McDonalds launched in Moscow, thirty thousand people queued up to get a taste of capitalist freedom. Sounds crazy today. You couldn't get three thousand out in the streets when their actual freedoms are taken away."

"Exactly. How did your date go, by the way? Have you finally met the girl of your dreams?"

"Her name is Magdalena. I haven't figured out what game she's playing, but things could get interesting."

"I can tell that something's bothering you. Your relationship didn't go off to a perfect start, did it?"

"It's called love at first sight. But it has nothing to do with romantic success. That's spy jargon for one of their recruitment techniques."

"Tell me what happened," Eugene said soberly.

"It was a cold approach. An all-round nice guy from the American Embassy asked me if I would be inclined to share certain information with him. I've been recruited by the CIA."

"You've got to be kidding me."

"I'm dead serious, Gene. Although it's somewhat ironic. Anyone who criticizes Frolov is accused of being an American spy. In my case, it might actually be true for a change."

"Do you think it could be a set-up?"

"The U.S. Embassy website has his mugshot and all. Stephen Hilton the Third seems to be a legit diplomat. Or at least someone operating under official diplomatic cover."

"So, what are you going to do?"

"I've been mulling over it, and my mind is set. I'm going to give Stephen the Third what he asks for. If the CIA wants to thwart the Kremlin's plans, I'll help in any way I can."

"I'm not sure I like the sound of it."

"Are you talking about my debt to the Motherland? Life deals each of us a hand. Birthplace is a card one cannot change, but it doesn't justify blind loyalty to a criminal government. I don't owe anything to the regime that's been killing Russia for the last hundred years. On the contrary, *not* fighting against it in any shape or form would be treason. You may be harboring doubts about my decision. It's perfectly understandable. But I'll do anything it takes to bring Frolov down. Even if it means siding with the devil, much less the CIA. There's no other way to win our country back, so I'm not going to be picky about my methods. Our Cossack ancestors, Adrian and Grigory Sokolov, faced a similar choice. Sometimes you need to ask yourself where you stand."

"I'm not here to judge you. I'll stand by you, even if we both end up in the wrong. But I still care about you, and I don't want you to get into trouble."

"We're in trouble already. There's no clearer indication of it than having Saveliy Frolov walk into the Kremlin."

"You know what I mean. You've never hesitated to throw yourself in harm's way, like the horror you went through in France."

"That was different. This time, we'll stick together. And besides, you should be more concerned about your own safety. Take Klimov, for example. I don't want you to suffer the same fate. It's better to resign than wait to be kicked out—or worse."

"I'm used to taking risks."

"A job as hazardous as yours makes it too easy to fake an accident. Without Klimov's protection, you'll simply get killed in the line of duty."

"I'll stick around. Saving innocent lives is more important than politics. I can't quit EMERCOM."

"EMERCOM may soon cease to exist, anyway," Constantine said.

"What is that supposed to mean?"

"Apparently, Frolov wants to disband it."

"We'll see about that. But this intel might have some legs. I've heard as much. This Hilton guy knows his stuff. He may not be lying, after all. What's he snooping into?"

"Frolov is plotting an act of terror in a major European city. If what Hilton says is true, the death toll would be staggering. And, Gene, I'm sorry to say this ... but Asiyah Kasymova could play a role in it."

"I knew she would come back to haunt me like a bad dream."

"You don't sound surprised to hear her name."

"I *saw* her. In the flesh. I never told you, but I spotted Asiyah Kasymova at the inauguration. So your CIA guy is right, at least on one count. What else did you learn?"

"He mentioned a top-secret military program. Allegedly, Frolov is prepared to reactivate it. I only know the code name. Mercury-18."

"Are you sure you got that right?"

"Absolutely."

Eugene's eyes filled with unease.

"What exactly is Mercury-18?" Constantine asked.

"I only have a vague idea. I'm not sure how much of it is grounded in fact. There are more questions than answers, and I'm no expert on the matter. But I know someone who can help us." Eugene flicked his wrist to glance at the Breitling chronometer. "We still have enough time to make it back before sunrise."

He rose sharply, reaching for the car key fob in his pocket.

"Where are we going?"

"Klimov's house. We must talk to him right away."

7

The *dacha* was situated between the luxury suburbs of Zhukovka and Barvikha, ten kilometers west of Moscow. By the standards of those ultra-rich communities and their affluent residents, Klimov's villa appeared modest. The four-bedroom, four-bathroom detached house sat on a half-acre land plot encircled by pine trees. All the other properties in the area were up for sale. Constantine was struck by the surrounding desolation.

Eugene navigated his Audi Q5 through the deserted alleys of what had virtually become a ghost town. Klimov's neighbors had fled overseas in the face of an imminent economic collapse that loomed over Russia, putting their houses on the market. There were hardly any takers for the toxic real estate. The opulent villas now stood as abandoned monuments of former petrodollar glory. Klimov, however, was a firm believer that a market crash was the perfect time to buy, not sell. He had no plans to leave the country, so the investment was worth a gamble if the Russian economy ever showed signs of recovery. If not, he'd still have a roof over his head.

"Ah, the Sokolov brothers," said Klimov as he welcomed them inside his new home. "Thanks for dropping by, although I must admit I didn't expect any visitors. I do appreciate your company, though. These short summer nights are giving me insomnia."

He led them into the living room of his bachelor pad. It was the first time either of them had been inside the house. Minimalist, with only metal, leather, and wooden surfaces, it was designed to provide comfort for a single man's lifestyle. The interior felt cozy and tidy despite the lack of a feminine touch. Constantine sank into a soft Chester armchair. On the coffee table, a gadget that looked like a wireless router drew Eugene's attention.

"What've you got here?" Eugene asked. "Free Wi-Fi?"

"Nothing of the sort. It's a white noise emitter."

"White noise?" Constantine echoed.

"A counter-surveillance tool," Eugene clarified as he approached the window and peered out. "Are you aware of a metallic-blue Renault hatchback parked across the road? Caught my eye as I was passing by. A couple of guys sitting inside."

"Yeah, I noticed them about a week ago. Some hapless FSB goons assigned to snoop on me. Two teams of wheel artists taking turns. The other car is a Nissan sedan. They don't bother concealing their presence. They're here for intimidation more than anything. Surveillance is pretty frustrating in my case. Anyway, better safe than sorry, so I'm using counter-measures. This little box renders any listening device useless. They'd need to beam a laser microphone at my window to capture any audio. But I'm too low-priority to warrant such expenses, which is a bit of a blow to my ego, to be honest. I also have a cell phone jammer powered up in the garage to make their job more miserable."

Eugene glanced at the screen of his rugged Sonim handset.

"No service."

"The signal is blocked within a one-mile radius. Thankfully I don't have to deal with the neighbors."

"So this room is safe from eavesdropping?"

"Ninety-nine percent secure. Don't worry."

"That's reassuring to hear. The topic we need to discuss is highly sensitive."

"If it's important enough to bring you here at this hour, I'm all ears. What do you want to talk about?"

"Mercury-18," Constantine said.

"Not the best choice of subject for academic research."

"But one I'm very much interested in."

"For what reason?"

"My interest is most practical. I want to know how to stop Mercury-18. Therefore, I also need to know how it works. So I need your expert opinion on both. For starters, can you confirm that it's real?"

"Certainly. Mercury-18 does exist. But it's irrelevant. The program has been shelved for some time, as far as I know."

"Not if President Frolov is preparing to dust it off."

"Your resignation has paved the way for him to access it."

Klimov waved his hand dismissively. "Even if he puts his own man in charge of EMERCOM—"

"He won't," Eugene interjected. "He'll get rid of EMERCOM altogether."

Klimov grimaced as if struck physically.

"According to my source, Frolov is eager to deploy Mercury-18 any time soon," Constantine said.

"Do you understand the implications?"

"That's why we're here."

"Either of you want a drink?"

"No, thanks."

"I'm driving."

"Well, I hope you don't mind. I definitely need a sedative right now. It's not every night that I discuss a Tesla superweapon."

The former head of EMERCOM was lost in thought as he opened the liquor cabinet. Constantine studied his face. The sacking had hit Klimov hard. A few extra gray strands had appeared in his salt-and-pepper hair. His strong jawline, normally clean-shaven, was dotted with silver stubble. His stare had become hollow.

Had he been on the booze? Unlikely. He'd never been a heavy drinker, and it would take a lot more to break him.

But still, his words made no sense.

Tesla?

Daniil Klimov's choice of sedative was a Macallan 12-year-old single malt whiskey. He poured a shot into a crystal tumbler and returned to his guests. After taking a long sip, Klimov spoke.

"For decades, the world has lived in fear of a nuclear holocaust. But imagine if a true weapon of the next world war had already been developed—more horrifying, more potent, more dangerous than any nuke. Untraceable and immune to counter-attack."

The preamble did grab Constantine's attention.

"How would this ultimate strike be carried out?"

"By targeting enemy territory with large-scale natural disasters."

"You're talking about—"

"Weather modification."

Constantine asked, "Do you mean that it's actually possible to control the weather?"

"Of course. The UN even addressed the issue way back in 1976, I believe, banning the military use of environmental modification techniques. It didn't keep the U.S. and the Soviet Union from developing electromagnetic weaponry to alter the ionosphere. The idea is hardly new, but it's taken the world's most brilliant minds and decades of scientific progress to make it possible."

"You mentioned Nikola Tesla. How does he fit in?" Constantine said with a hint of skepticism in his voice.

"Always ahead of his time, he was the man who devised the concept. After Tesla's death, there was a scramble for his secrets. The FBI seized boxes full of his research papers, but they never found what they were looking for. The missing documents were located in Belgrade, so Tesla's most crucial work fell into Soviet hands after the Second World War. His genius laid the groundwork for the future of warfare. Or perhaps I should say modern warfare. Today, weather-modification facilities have already been built."

"Such as the American HAARP installations? Only lunatics believe in HAARP's weather engineering capabilities."

"Perhaps. I can't vouch for the results of U.S. efforts in the field. What I do know is that the Russian weather-control system no longer belongs to the realm of science fiction. It's called scalar electromagnetic technology and it's fully functional. Have you noticed any strange weather patterns around the world lately?"

"Sure," Eugene said. "There have been hailstorms in Israel and Texas, flash flooding in Great Britain, and forest fires across Europe."

"Are you suggesting that all this freak weather is man-made?" Constantine asked.

"No doubt. All that bullshit like global warming has nothing to do with it." Klimov smirked. "The bizarre weather conditions are generated by transmitters known as Woodpeckers. They emit Extreme Low Frequency signals at ten Hertz which affect high-altitude jet streams. While testing the Woodpeckers, Soviet scientists learned how to create either massive flooding, or droughts that could last indefinitely. Later, they conducted experiments to manipulate weather on a global scale. They can direct storms, tornadoes, floods, or wildfires anywhere in the world, at any time, on a whim. It's the perfect weapon for anyone who wants to play God."

"Is there any evidence to support these claims?"

"The Americans discovered an array of old Woodpecker transmitters in Ukraine, so they're fully aware of the destructive potential. Officially, however, the U.S. can't prove that Russia is still operating weather-control facilities. There are several of them scattered around Russia. The mammoth *Sura* complex near Nizhny Novgorod, and another ELF station near Murmansk are well-known to foreign intelligence.

As you understand, the sites are off limits, so freak weather can't be directly linked to their activity."

"What about Mercury-18?"

"It's the next stage of environmental warfare. The geophysical WMD research didn't stop at the ionosphere. The Woodpecker program, no matter how successful, was just the beginning. A peashooter compared to the howitzer of Mercury-18."

"Hold on," said Constantine. "There's something even more powerful than electromagnetic weather altering?"

"Yes. The energy of the Earth's core. Releasing it would cripple nations or even entire continents."

"Bloody hell."

"That's exactly what Mercury-18 is supposed to bring about. Hell on Earth. It's a technology to trigger earthquakes. A tectonic weapon aimed at the Earth's lithosphere."

His brother had been right. Constantine would never have believed what he'd just heard if it wasn't coming from a top-level government source.

"Does it actually work?"

"Indeed, it's quite advanced. So much that Mercury-18 testing has led to a few international incidents. In 2002 the Kremlin was accused of causing a Magnitude Six earthquake in the Republic of Georgia by that country's Green Party leader. And in 1997, the Chechens thwarted an FSB plan to use tectonic weapons against Grozny. This is just the tip of the iceberg. Development of the tectonic bomb began in the 1970s and was pretty much complete by 1990."

Constantine shook his head incredulously. "How many people are in the know?"

"Only a handful inside the government. Tectonic weapons research is highly classified, and Mercury-18 is perhaps the most secret military program of them all. EMERCOM is looking out for unusual seismic activity that could be related to it, but only those with maximum clearance have access to the full details."

"Is it available for use by the new President ...?"

The gravity of his final question lingered in the air.

Constantine saw the real reason behind Klimov's sleepless nights. It was not the loss of status that was gnawing at him, not even the danger to his personal safety, but a sense of foreboding that gripped them all. A shadow of impending doom. And now it had a name, first spelled out by Stephen Hilton III.

Mercury-18.

8

A blushing sliver of dawn crept across the sky as the Audi Q5 charged along the highway, heading back to Moscow. The gentle murmur of the two-liter turbo engine was the loudest sound inside the car as they drove in brooding silence. Constantine contemplated Klimov's revelations.

A siren blared from behind. In the rearview mirror, Constantine glimpsed a police cruiser tailing them, lights flashing.

"What the hell?" he muttered.

"No idea. I swear I wasn't speeding."

"Could be anything, then. Damn."

The Russian police force ranked as one of the world's most corrupt. The encounter promised nothing but trouble. As Eugene pulled over, Constantine braced himself for a grueling extortion session.

The police car, a Toyota Camry, pulled behind. Two uniformed cops got out. One of them, a beer-bellied lieutenant, approached the Audi. The other officer, thin and red-faced, stayed behind and drew his gun, a Makarov PM.

"Keep your cool," Eugene told his brother. "Don't let them bait you."

He rolled the window a quarter of the way down and placed his hands on the steering wheel.

As the policeman leaned forward, the stench of sweat and garlic drifted through the narrow window slit.

"Where are you headed to?" he demanded. He spoke with a thick provincial accent, from somewhere beyond the Urals, the dialect as crude as the mountains. Lowlifes from all over the country flocked to Moscow in search of easy money, and many joined the police for the salary and benefits—as well as the power that came with the badge.

Eugene ignored the question.

"What's the problem, chief? Any reason for the stop?"

"Just a routine check. Your car matches the description of one involved in a robbery. You guys also fit the profile of the suspects. I need to verify your identities."

Eugene offered his driver's license.

"Sokolov," the cop read out, snatching it from his fingers. "What about your passenger over there?"

Constantine passed his own ID card to the lieutenant.

As he examined it, the cop's flabby mug twisted in a scowl. He keyed his walkie-talkie. Constantine couldn't make out what he was mumbling into it. A garbled voice hissed through the static in return.

When he finished, the cop moved his hand to unlatch the hip holster.

"Turn off the engine and leave the vehicle," the cop commanded.

Eugene did as ordered.

"Now you!" the cop shouted to Constantine. "Out! Place your hands on the roof!"

The lieutenant gestured to his partner, pointing at Constantine. The other cop marched forward, pistol aimed.

"Open the trunk," the obese officer told Eugene. Complying, he pressed a button on the key fob and the Audi's rear door lifted automatically.

The lieutenant made a perfunctory search. Obviously, he knew there was nothing to be found inside the Q5. Why go through with the farce, then? Constantine kept a keen eye on his motions to ensure that the fat cop didn't plant anything inside the car. Placing a tiny bag of heroin was standard practice for a frame.

Minutes passed. No, they weren't extorting a bribe. The cops were stalling time, holding them up for whatever reason. Constantine didn't like it one bit.

His misgivings materialized as a silver Ford Transit van pulled beside the police cruiser.

The side door of the van flew open and a group of four men spilled out. AK rifles, armored vests, unmarked combat uniforms, and balaclavas. Rapidly, they positioned themselves around the Audi. Lacking any insignia, they reminded Constantine of the special forces members who had taken over Crimea.

The two policemen appeared unperturbed by the arrival of masked soldiers. If nothing else, the cops had been expecting them.

The last man leaped out of the Ford Transit. He had an unremarkable physique, but he compensated for his average height and build with a tactical vest and an AK rifle slung over his shoulder. Likewise, his camouflage uniform bore no insignia, but he wasn't hiding his face. A butch cut blended his receding hairline with his goatee. A physiognomist would have a field day with the facial features: fleshy lips, an upturned nose, and heavy brow ridges protruding over a pair of narrow eyes. The stare was menacing. Clearly, he was the one in charge of the whole operation.

"What do you want?" Eugene addressed him in an ice-cool voice.

"Major Sokolov, this is an emergency. You're required to report for duty at once. We're under orders to accompany you to the EMERCOM airbase. Follow me."

Constantine and his brother exchanged understanding glances. No time for heroics. Wordlessly, Eugene proceeded to the van under armed escort. No sooner had the door slammed shut than the van drove off, whipping up a trail of dust in its wake.

As the Ford sped away, Constantine observed the receding taillights with growing despair. It had been a set-up, all right, leading into a trap. The policemen had acted as errand boys in a kidnapping.

He winced as the two cops twisted his arms, cuffed his wrists behind his back, and shoved him toward the Toyota.

9

Eugene Sokolov entertained no illusion about his chances to overpower five heavily-armed special forces members in the confines of the van. He had to size up the situation before he could act. The long drive gave him ample time to analyze his predicament. The raid had been pre-planned and swiftly executed. Russian black-ops teams specialized in cross-border abductions, applying similar tactics. They effectively held him prisoner. For extra leverage, his brother was still detained by the police. He was powerless to do anything about it, for now. He would have to be patient, and wait for an opportunity to present itself.

The EMERCOM airfield was based in the town of Zhukovsky, twenty-five kilometers southeast of Moscow. Sokolov determined that the van was bound south*west*. Destination unknown.

Sandwiched between two balaclava-wearing guards, he turned to their apish leader.

"What sort of emergency brings me the pleasure of your company? You never introduced yourself, by the way."

"All in due course, Major. Don't ask too many questions, for your own sake," the ape replied with a sadistic grin. "And your brother's."

A tense silence grew. Constantine's disquieting words flashed through his mind.

"A job as hazardous as yours makes it too easy to fake an accident. Without Klimov's protection, you'll simply get killed in the line of duty."

He'd never expected the moment to come so soon, but he'd be damned if he let them do it. He hoped to prove his brother wrong—and to see him again, safe and sound, as soon as possible.

The Ford Transit veered off to a side road cutting through forest and reached a seemingly endless concrete fence topped by barbed wire. The van halted at a roadblock before a massive gate. A sign read: RESTRICTED AREA.

Seconds later, the gate rumbled open.

A lone security guard in military uniform waved them through without so much as a cursory inspection of the vehicle or its occupants. Obviously, the van had passed the checkpoint numerous times, and was treated as one of their own.

Sokolov scanned the surroundings. It was an airbase, after all. Only EMERCOM had nothing to do with it. He found himself in Kubinka, home of the 45th Airborne Reconnaissance Brigade, Spetsnaz GRU. Established in 1994, the brigade had gained notoriety for the kidnapping and torture of Chechen civilians. Sabotage missions during the invasion of Ukraine had cemented their reputation as tough, ruthless bastards.

The Ford stopped in front of an aircraft hangar. His abductors convoyed Sokolov inside. It housed an Ilyushin Il-76 cargo jet, an orange-and-blue EMERCOM strip running across its white airframe. The odor of a fresh coat of paint lingered in the air. The hastily-done paint job, while not one hundred percent accurate, came pretty damn close to the real thing. A layman would never spot the fake.

Equally fake was the airplane's crew. A trio of ruffians was idling away in foul-mouthed chatter. They were dressed in blue coveralls bearing the EMERCOM eight-pointed star crests. Thuggish-looking with their low foreheads and glowering stares, they could model for a Spetsnaz recruitment poster.

The fourth crew member was the plane's loadmaster. A forklift was carrying a pallet with a stack of boxes restrained by netting, while he directed it into the cargo hold of the Ilyushin.

A GRU officer in the rank of colonel oversaw the proceedings. His olive-skinned face was beaded with perspiration below his flight cap and around his pencil-thin mustache. He was clutching a brown leather briefcase.

"Hurry up, Umar!" he yelled to the loadmaster.

Umar yelled something back in what Sokolov recognized as a Central Asian dialect.

Seeing the group of operators enter the hangar, the colonel extracted a manila envelope from his briefcase and handed it to the team leader.

"The documents are in order. You're good to go."

"Thank you, comrade *zampolit*," he said, taking it.

He produced a green-colored passport and thumbed through it, studying the pages carefully.

"Let's see. Hmmm ... *Vladislav Panin*. You wanted a name for me, you got it, Major." He winked at Sokolov. Then he waved the passport at the colonel. "Rhymes with Vladimir Lenin. Tell those Foreign Ministry boys to get a bit more imaginative next time, okay?"

Then he retrieved another passport from the folder and gave it to Sokolov.

It was a Russian diplomatic passport. Green cover with gold printing. Most likely genuine, issued by the Ministry of Foreign Affairs in his own name and carrying his photo. Freshly printed, the pristine pages bore no stamps.

"To answer your previous question, Major Sokolov, you'll be required to do your job. The kind that justifies your paychecks. Delivery of humanitarian aid. A standard EMERCOM mission to help those in need."

"Okay, Vlad. Which country has the misfortune to require your help?"

"One that you're quite familiar with. Germany. They just don't know about it yet. But first, we'll have to make a small detour."

10

The main freight deck of the Ilyushin was equipped with jump seats. Like he'd done numerous times flying aboard a cargo plane, Sokolov sat in trancelike meditation, eyes closed. He mentally shut off the screaming sound of the four turbofan engines, but his sensory awareness tuned to pick up the earliest sign of danger coming from Panin, who sat next to him.

His mind transported him years back, to the country of his childhood. His family had lived at a Soviet Air Force base in Magdeburg, East Germany. Even on the wrong side of the Iron Curtain, it had been Germany all the same, a land vastly different from Russia. Only years later had he realized that his father, a MiG pilot, had been part of an occupation force. What would his father have done during a Soviet invasion of Western Europe? He'd remained a mystery even to his own sons. Deep down, he'd despised the Soviet regime. Perhaps he'd joined the Red Army hoping for a possible defection. Instead of fighting for communism, he'd wanted his family to escape it. Whether or not he'd been wrestling with his conscience, it had become irrelevant with the fall of the Berlin Wall. In the end, he'd returned with his family to Russia, and it was the Russian army that had killed him.

Moscow had always felt alien to Eugene Sokolov, even more so after claiming his father's life. While Germany had never been his *Rodina* or *Fatherland*, he had always felt a spiritual connection with it. There was a German word for it. *Heimat.* It had no substitute in any other language. A metaphysical concept that tugged at his heartstrings, filling him with a sense of belonging.

Yeah, sometimes you had to ask yourself where you stood. And now, as the GRU spearheaded a covert invasion, he most certainly did. Spetsnaz troops were assigned with only the blackest of black ops. Their job was murder and destruction, while Sokolov's was the exact opposite. He didn't know their objective, but the reason for the EMERCOM cover became apparent three hours later when they made the stopover.

With a jolt, the plane touched down at an airfield in Niš, Serbia. Ironically enough, it was called Constantine the Great Airport. Apart from servicing local air traffic, it also housed EMERCOM's single base located outside Russia.

Sokolov didn't share the same sentiments for Serbia as he had for Germany, despite the fact that some of his ancestors had fled to Belgrade following the Revolution. As an ethnic Cossack, he didn't believe in pan-Slavic unity. Helping out the Balkan brethren had always proved more trouble than it was worth, as evidenced by the First World War. And after the Second, the Balkans had become a communist stronghold under Tito's iron-fisted rule. Much like the USSR, Yugoslavia had been an artificial country held together by a dictatorship. Without it, the Yugoslav republics had broken away from Serbia, fighting for their freedom and independence in the bloodiest wars the European continent had seen in years. When NATO forces halted the genocide of Albanian Muslims in Kosovo, leading to the downfall of Slobodan Milošević, the Kremlin had lost one of its oldest allies. The President's arrest had come as a shock to his Moscow backers, themselves former commies-turned-nationalists who'd perpetrated war crimes in Chechnya. Since then, a deep-rooted fear of suffering the same fate had been fueling the Kremlin's phobia of NATO.

Bitter nationalism had kept the Serbs from following

their neighbors on the road to EU membership, and Moscow exploited it, gaining influence and support. *Kosovo is Serbia, Crimea is Russia!* The slogan spread like wildfire.

The Kremlin still viewed Serbia as a springboard for meddling in Balkan affairs. Montenegro had recently foiled a coup d'état aimed against the country's bid to join NATO. A group of Serbian and Russian militants had planned to assassinate the Montenegrin Prime Minister, overthrow the parliament, and bring a pro-Kremlin party into power.

To maintain a firm grasp on Serbia in a geopolitical tug-of-war, the Kremlin's reach extended in devious ways. In 2012, Russia set up an EMERCOM disaster relief facility in the town of Niš. Officially called the Russian-Serbian Humanitarian Center, it was supposed to coordinate joint efforts in firefighting, flood relief, and demining. Whether the functions included espionage was anybody's guess. Sokolov did know one thing for certain. According to the agreement with the Serbs, all EMERCOM cargo arriving in Niš was entitled to diplomatic immunity.

That included the freight delivered by the Spetsnaz hitmen.

The Ilyushin taxied briefly before coming to a stop. The whine of the engines flooded inside as the rear clamshell doors of the cargo compartment opened.

"Welcome to brotherly Serbia." Panin produced a sheet of paper from his manila envelope and shoved it to Sokolov—along with a pen. "Sign here."

It was an airway bill, listing humanitarian goods as the cargo: clothes, shoes, blankets, medical supplies. No doubt the real contents of those boxes were far more dangerous.

"And if I don't?"

"You'll either sign the airway bill or your brother's death warrant. I'm not here to play games."

Sokolov clutched the ballpoint pen, resisting the urge to ram it into Panin's eye or windpipe. His anger wouldn't solve anything—yet. Panin knew it, too.

Sokolov scribbled his name at the bottom of the page. Signing the airway bill off, he took full responsibility for the shipment. Panin was using him as a screen and ensuring his silence.

He gave him another sheet. "Two copies. You can keep the duplicate."

The GRU man wasn't playing a game—he thought he'd already won it.

11

The sky was hazy from the distant forest fires raging somewhere beyond the low hills surrounding Niš. The smoke was hanging like a veil, obscuring the sunlight.

Working as a well-drilled unit, the GRU goons removed the net off the pallet and began offloading the cargo. Sokolov got his first real look at the boxes. Most of them appeared similar to cartons used for relief supplies packaging—but not all. Hidden among them were green-painted crates that looked like they'd freshly come off a small arms factory conveyor belt. He counted a dozen of those, coming in two sizes.

Sokolov took note of the markings on a couple of larger, elongated crates: *6P1 - 5pcs - 27kg*. According to the Russian Ministry of Defense indices, 6P1 stood for Kalashnikov rifles. The ten smaller ones, labeled 57-N-231, were crammed with 7.62mm ammunition, 920 rounds per box. As someone familiar with the munition designation codes, he knew it instantly.

The crates were being transferred to a medium-sized Ford Cargo truck waiting on the tarmac. Sokolov made a mental note of the truck's license plate.

There wasn't a single security or customs officer in sight. Instead, a Russian-made Lada Niva was heading toward the Ilyushin. The vehicle braked sharply as it reached the apron. A young man in EMERCOM uniform got out from behind the wheel and strode across the tarmac.

"Major Sokolov?"

Sokolov flashed his EMERCOM ID badge.

"Lieutenant Matvei Rykov," the young man said, offering his hand.

Sokolov shook it.

"Glad you made it here, Major," said Rykov. "The fires have been pretty bad. A lot of people have been affected in the nearby villages. We can use any help we can get, and having someone like you around, with your skill and experience, is a massive boost."

Sokolov studied the young officer. A broad, weathered face, wavy black hair, and brown eyes that had witnessed enough to make him appear a few years older than he really was.

Would he risk telling him about Panin and the GRU operation? Sokolov weighed the options. What if Rykov, too, was an undercover Spetsnaz officer? What if that EMERCOM center had been set up in the first place as a front for GRU activities? If not, then exposing the secret mission would put both of their lives on the line. Either way, Sokolov didn't want to get himself killed on the spot by Panin's goons. Glancing over his shoulder, he saw that they would finish loading the truck before long. The Ford's diesel rumbled, idling. He had to play his cards right.

Rykov broke his reverie.

"May I have the airway bill? I need to hand it in to the Serbs with the rest of the paperwork."

"The formalities can wait. Where's your boss?"

On paper, the Russian-Serbian Humanitarian Center was headed by a Serbian official, but in fact it was the Russian co-director running the show.

"Uh, he's still at the office. It's just around the corner, literally a five-minute walk from here."

"Five minutes won't cut it. Hit the accelerator."

"All right," Rykov said reluctantly. "Get in, Major."

Rykov turned the ignition and the Lada coughed up exhaust fumes. No sooner had Sokolov climbed in the front passenger seat than the Lada lurched forward. The lieutenant threw the lumbering car into a curve around the terminal, reaching the chain-link fence of the airport perimeter. Stopping to show his pass to a security guard, the lieutenant drove through the gate and put on a spurt along the five-hundred-meter stretch of the road leading to the Center, arriving in under sixty seconds.

The Humanitarian Center took up two identical, adjacent buildings: the headquarters and the warehouse. Both were hideous cuboid monoliths, painted black and almost windowless.

Rykov led Sokolov into the headquarters, past the empty lobby and conference room, walking straight into the co-director's office.

The office was standard fare: Serbian and Russian flags, a wall-mounted map of Serbia, a framed portrait of President Frolov, and a large window overlooking the airport.

Colonel Vasily Lisovsky, dressed in a civilian suit-and-tie outfit in lieu of an EMERCOM uniform, was sitting behind his desk, shifting his gaze between his laptop screen and a bank of monitors showing direct video feeds from the firefighting efforts in different locations.

The colonel had close-cropped gray hair, a clean-shaven face and bushy black eyebrows that arched aggressively. Sokolov had never met Lisovsky before. Friend or foe? There was only one way to find out.

"If I were you, Colonel, I'd turn my attention to the Il-76 outside."

Lisovsky gave him a cold stare.

"Sokolov, right? Sorry I didn't roll out the red carpet and greet you personally, Sokolov. You see, I'm busy doing my actual job, dealing with the damned forest fires."

"The damned forest fires might become the least of your worries."

"What the hell do you mean?"

Sokolov slammed the airway bill atop Lisovsky's desk. "This."

The colonel took a moment to study the document.

"What about it?"

"I have every reason to believe, Colonel, that the cargo delivered by the Ilyushin has nothing to do with the specified list."

"Care to elaborate, Major?"

"A group of Spetsnaz operatives has brought in a cache of weapons disguised as EMERCOM aid delivery."

"Pardon me for being blunt, but you need to have your head checked. Or your bloodstream."

"I saw it with my own eyes, Colonel. Don't act like it's never happened before. The Kremlin has illegally supplied weapons hidden as humanitarian cargo during every conflict from the Spanish Civil War to the invasion of Ukraine."

"So what? Why'd anybody want to do it here?"

"A GRU officer, alias Panin, is trying to smuggle the firearms into Germany. You know that the shortest route into the EU is via the Hungarian border. A truck loaded with the weapons will be on its way there any minute now."

"What are you going to tell me next? Did the Kremlin artificially cause these wildfires by some sort of weather machines?" Lisovsky's gravelly voice was laced with acid.

You have no idea, Sokolov thought. *Or do you?*

Lisovsky puffed his cheeks and let out a deep breath. "Major Sokolov, I don't know anyone named Panin. Do you have any real evidence? All I see is *your* signature on this document. It's *your* cargo, your men, and your plane. What point are you trying to make? You'll bring nothing but trouble upon yourself with these mad claims."

"I'm ready to face the consequences. A criminal investigation, if need be."

"What am I supposed to do about your conspiracy theory?"

"Panin must be stopped. Send your men after him before he gets away. Alert the Serbian authorities."

"Hold your horses. It ain't Moscow here. I don't have enough manpower. The Humanitarian Center is staffed by eight men. Three Serbs and four Russians—five, myself included. And all of them are out there together with the Serbian authorities, their hands full rescuing civilians. You want me to disrupt their work on your whim? And make a fool of myself in the process? I strongly believed that you were flying in to assist us, but it seems that I was mistaken."

"No disrespect, Colonel, but arresting that shipment is far more important. I don't need your permission to act alone."

"I've heard you're a maverick. I'm having none of that. Here in Niš, you're playing by my rules. Find something productive to do and stop overreacting. Rykov!"

"Yes, Comrade General?"

"Did you get a look at those crates? Anything suspicious about them?"

"No mystery here, Comrade Colonel. The Russian Strategic Reserves use the same kind of crates for storage of relief supplies. Maybe that's what got Major Sokolov confused. I think we have a few in the warehouse, left over from the previous shipment, unopened."

"Mind if I check them out?" Sokolov inquired.

"Be my guest," said Lisovsky. "Lieutenant Rykov! Give our guest a tour of the warehouse, will you?"

"My pleasure."

"This conversation is over, Major."

Sokolov stormed out of Lisovsky's office. Behind the emotional façade, he considered the meeting a success. He'd never expected Lisovsky to cooperate, but now he had a sense of the stuff Lisovsky was made of.

Sokolov knew where the lines were drawn and how the odds were stacked.

Nothing held him back from making his move.

12

Sokolov stepped into the darkness of the warehouse. Rykov hit a switch and ceiling lamps came on, flickering one by one to bathe the massive storage area in fluorescent glow.

The aisles were uncategorized. There was no semblance of logic to the placement of the supplies and lifesaving equipment. Rows of carton boxes alternated with heaps of mattresses, camping tent bundles, a jumble of folding tables and chairs. Three red-colored rubber boats were positioned side by side on the concrete floor. The warehouse doubled as a garage, with another Lada Niva and an ambulance parked inside.

"How do you find your way around this mess?" Sokolov asked.

"Go straight ahead. You'll spot the crates behind the ambulance."

Sokolov traversed the length of the warehouse, passing a pile of diving wetsuits, life vests, safety helmets, and mountain climbing gear. He kept a mental inventory of the items he saw, familiarizing himself with the layout of the warehouse. When Sokolov reached the ambulance, he saw nothing but empty space between the vehicle and the garage door. The military crates were missing—if they had ever been there.

"Now what?" Sokolov muttered.

"Now we send your body home in a body bag."

In a blur of motion, Rykov struck, the glint of a knife blade arcing toward Sokolov's neck.

Sokolov found himself cornered—but not outwitted. Anticipating the attack, he dodged the sweeping knife edge, which glanced off the side of the ambulance. He locked Rykov's wrist in a vise-like grip and wrenched the forearm. As Rykov lost his balance, Sokolov's knee rocketed up and smashed into the elbow joint, breaking it. Rykov yelled in agony, crashing down, his busted arm dangling. The knife clinked as it hit the hard floor.

"That'll teach you," Sokolov said. "Trying to sever someone's carotid artery isn't nice, Rykov. Is that your real name, anyway? Decent knife, though."

He picked it up. It was a Katran tactical knife. The serrated seven-inch blade made it equally useful for diving, combat, and survival missions. It was a limited edition favored by both EMERCOM and Spetsnaz officers. Sokolov owned one, too.

Sokolov slid open the side door of the ambulance.

"Get in, lieutenant. The hospital is just around the corner."

Rykov, or whoever he was, did not appreciate Sokolov's humor. Seething, he infused his groans with a few choice obscenities.

Sokolov's plan had worked. He'd forced their hand by confronting Lisovsky. But he wasn't out of the woods yet. Rykov's backup team couldn't be far away–and they would have been alerted by the man's cries.

Just then, the garage door swung upward, lifted by someone outside.

"He's right here!" Rykov shouted, struggling to get to his feet, overcoming the pain. "Kill him! Kill—"

The words froze in his throat, the Katran's blade penetrating it to the hilt.

Three members of the Ilyushin crew burst into warehouse, guns drawn and ready to fire. Sokolov was facing them like a target in a shooting gallery. The GRU hitmen had him dead to rights.

It was by luck or divine prescience that the ambulance door was already open, saving him the split-second needed to cheat death. Sokolov dived through the opening just as a fusillade of shots whizzed through the air where he should have been.

The bullets pierced the body of the ambulance and punched cracks in the windshield. Sokolov pushed the rear doors open and jumped out, hitting the floor in a roll.

He found cover behind the rubber hull of an inflatable boat. Reaching inside, he grabbed what he needed: a pack of hand-held distress signals and a flare gun.

He plucked the cords from all three flare tubes and tossed them aside. They emitted orange smoke that began to fill the warehouse.

Searching for him, the first GRU hitman emerged from behind the ambulance. Seeing Sokolov hiding behind the boat, he squeezed off several shots.

The boat hissed, leaking air through the punctures in its PVC-coated skin. Sokolov pulled the trigger of the flare gun and the scorching projectile streaked into the Spetsnaz pilot's torso. He toppled, screaming.

His two partners came right behind him, guns blazing.

Too late. They were shooting wildly through the orange mist. The smoke screen from the distress signals shrouded Sokolov completely.

He moved quickly, having obtained another object from the bullet-riddled boat. An oar.

Sokolov's top-level mastery of karate had acquainted him with the rare art of Eku Bo. It was the fighting style of Okinawan fishermen who had turned their oars into devastating weapons. He didn't consider himself an expert practitioner, and the aluminum oar was a far cry from the traditional Eku, but any advantage counted when it came down to life and death.

The orange haze was impregnable, as if a real forest fire were raging within the warehouse.

The first man was shrieking. Embedded in the wound, the pyrotechnic missile had incinerated the flesh around it, burning intensely for seven seconds.

"I'm hit! Do something!"

"Shut up!" another voice snarled.

"You see him, Tolstoy?" asked the third killer.

Sokolov's keen hearing never failed him. With the stealth of a wraith, he crept through the cloud of acrid smoke. Wielding the shaft in a chopping motion, he brought the heavy edge of the oar spoon against Tolstoy's temple. The bone cracked, and he collapsed, dead.

Sokolov snatched his gun and fired point-blank at the murky silhouette of the other Spetsnaz killer.

The body jerked as the slugs tore into it, blood gushing. Sokolov fired again to finish him off.

The only audible sound was the wail of the man hit by the flare, left sprawled on the floor by his comrades.

Mercifully, Sokolov put him out of his misery by blasting a hole through the back of his skull.

Sokolov slipped out of the warehouse through the garage door. Filling his lungs with fresh air, he checked the pistol—a sleek, black Glock 17. Five rounds remained. He snapped the magazine back in and returned to Lisovsky's office.

13

As Sokolov walked through his door, Colonel Lisovsky did not even look up from the laptop screen.

"Did you get rid of him?" he asked absently. "Where's the body?"

"That's four bodies," Sokolov said. "Five, yourself included."

Lisovsky's eyes grew in horror, locking on Sokolov. Mouth agape, he yanked a desk drawer open and groped for something inside. Whether he was retrieving a gun or mashing a panic button, the attempt ended in futility. His starched white shirt bloomed with red blotches as a pair of 9mm bullets from the Glock hit him in the chest.

Lisovsky sagged in the chair, his lifeless stare confirming the five-man kill count.

Sokolov inspected the desk. Sure enough, the open drawer contained a Yarygin MP-443 semiautomatic, engraved with Lisovsky's name, and a box of rounds. Glock and Yarygin handguns were procured by the GRU, as well as EMERCOM, so Sokolov knew one when he saw one. He left the Yarygin untouched, but took the ammo. Both models used the 9x19mm Parabellum cartridges. As Sokolov reloaded the Glock to full 17-round capacity, his mind raced.

He assessed the situation with ice-cold calm, as though he were in the middle of a rescue operation. Assisted by two local undercover GRU officers, the Spetsnaz team had attempted to murder him and transport his body back to Moscow aboard the Ilyushin. Now they were dead, but

Sokolov could ill afford to drop his guard. He was still on hostile ground. Panin and Umar—also a trained killer—were out there somewhere.

His first objective was evacuation. He would be unable to hijack the Ilyushin to Moscow, but neither could he hang around long enough for the Serbian authorities to apprehend him.

He eyed the video displays on Lisovsky's desk. An airport surveillance camera showed the apron area where the Ilyushin was parked. There was zero activity around it. The big freight plane looked forsaken. The truck had vanished.

Was it heading to the warehouse?

All EMERCOM vehicles were equipped with GLONASS tracking devices, providing live data to the command center in Moscow. A shot in the dark, but with the system monitoring more than 25,000 vehicles in real time, it was worth a try. Sokolov seized the rugged, blood-spill-resistant laptop and launched a browser, logging into the secure portal. The online interface offered him a map of Russia and Europe. From memory, he typed the truck's license plate number into a search box and hit *Enter*. He wasn't holding his breath for any results, but the map zoomed in on southern Serbia. A blinking dot was moving along the A4 highway, south of Niš.

All clear. Now to get the hell out of there.

He quit the Web interface and the view switched back to the email app. He read the conversation which had captivated Lisovsky so much that it had cost him his life.

Fwd: Berlin

GULFSTREAM flying in today.

He scrolled through the message thread until he came across the attached image.

It showed a scan of a Serbian passport. Neither the name nor the nationality meant anything. Only the photo did. It was Asiyah Kasymova.

Even a grainy picture of her face stirred a whirlwind of emotions inside him.

Why, dammit! That photo squashed all hope, no matter how faint, that she had nothing to do with any of it. The proof was beyond doubt.

He'd told Lisovsky that Panin had to be stopped. Now more than ever he was determined to do it—and he was the only man capable of thwarting the conspiracy. A conspiracy so far-reaching and deadly that he couldn't back out of the job. What he'd encountered was just the tip of the iceberg. It ran much deeper than just a simple arms-smuggling operation. The true scope of the plot was beyond his grasp, but the events so far had lent chilling credence to Constantine's theory.

Sokolov knew nothing of his brother's fate. He still had to deal with Panin to ensure Constantine's safety. He *had* to reach Germany—fast. The time frame was too narrow. The route wouldn't take Panin more than several hours. The truck was moving south, toward the Bulgarian border. Once the cargo was smuggled into EU territory, it could be flown in directly from Sofia. And Asiyah Kasymova was already en route to Berlin Schönefeld Airport. Whatever their plan was, Sokolov had to get there and find either Panin or Asiyah.

He searched the desk for the laptop case. Before he found it, a bigger prize fell to him. The bottom drawer was filled to the brim with wads of money. At least fifty thousand Euros in hundred-Euro notes. Sokolov threw the laptop into the case, and crammed ten thousand Euros around its compartments. Slinging the case over his shoulder, Glock in hand, he departed the office for the warehouse once more.

The smoke had cleared, discharging through the open garage door and the building's ventilation system. Ignoring the corpses lying in pools of blood, Sokolov went on with his business. He unzipped an empty backpack and filled it with essentials.

Emergency four-ounce drinking water packets. Energy bars. A personal hygiene pack. An LED flashlight. A sleeping bag. Binoculars. A first aid kit from the ambulance.

Finally, he addressed the issue of his blood-stained EMERCOM uniform. He cut open several carton boxes of humanitarian aid marked as clothing. He found a checkered shirt, faded jeans, and sneakers that just about fit and seemed reasonably clean. He quickly changed, and stuffed spare shirts, socks, underwear, and a Colorado Avalanche hat into the bag. He had no qualms about dressing in old and shabby clothes. It was the perfect camouflage. He only felt sorry about taking clothes donated for those in desperate need, but he himself fell into that category at the moment, and none of the items were going to reach their intended recipients anyway.

When he was done, he threw the backpack over his shoulder, abandoned the warehouse, and marched five hundred meters along the road toward Constantine the Great Airport. Along the way, he disposed of the Glock, breaking it down and plunking the separate parts into the nearest storm drain.

He entered the compact but well-maintained terminal. Low-cost carriers operated three or four daily flights to a handful of European destinations. He checked the Departures board.

Eindhoven. Bratislava. Basel.

The day's last flight was scheduled at 15:30.

Berlin (SXF). Schönefeld.

Approaching the sales booth, he flashed his best smile to the dark-haired female agent behind the counter. She didn't give a second look to his outfit, typical of solo travelers, but her eyes, messy with flakes of old mascara, betrayed curiosity when Sokolov presented his diplomatic passport.

Promptly, he paid the fare by cash, and proceeded to the check-in area.

Standing in the bus queue to board the Boeing 737-800, Sokolov braced himself for a long two hours of the no-frills trip. Physically, the fatigue of the last couple of days was catching up with him. Mentally, he couldn't wait to land in Berlin. He was pondering his next move.

He envisaged the encounter with Asiyah Kasymova. Was she a victim or a willing accomplice?

He'd get his answers.

He'd saved her life once. If she betrayed him, he vowed not to make the same mistake again.

14

Butyrka prison. A fortress originally built during the reign of Catherine the Great to incarcerate criminals on their way to Siberian exile. Only when one of Butyrka's inmates, Felix Dzerzhinsky, had come to power did its sinister reputation grow. Through the years of communist terror, Butyrka had become synonymous with pain, suffering, and misery as a hellground for tens of thousands of new Russian martyrs. Today, it was Moscow's largest remand jail where detainees were held as they faced trial.

Constantine had no memory of getting admitted there, having his fingerprints taken, being strip-searched, or ending up where he was now.

He was inside a crypt-like cell measuring three by four feet.

He'd been placed there several hours ago—he couldn't tell how long exactly, because the prison guards had confiscated his wristwatch.

Total darkness. No water or food. No motion in the tight confines. A hole in the floor to relieve bodily needs. His limbs felt weak, so he pressed against a wall and sank to a narrow bench protruding from it. Apart from standing upright, it was the only position that was possible in the constricted space.

The physical discomfort added to the psychological pressure.

In the first few hours, he'd maintained self-control, thinking rationally. His predicament was hardly unique. He summoned all of his knowledge of the Butyrka from firsthand accounts, including those written by Solzhenitsyn and Shalamov.

The crypt was a blackout cell where remand prisoners were kept in transit to or from the main block. Why the sadistic ordeal was necessary every time a detainee was moved between the courthouse, interrogation room or visiting area, Constantine had no clue.

Then he recalled the morbid function of these crypts during Stalin's Great Terror. A Buturka inmate was transferred here before imminent execution by a firing squad. The fact did little to alleviate his mounting panic.

Hours passed—was it six or eight now? In the back of his mind, a seed of apprehension grew into an all-encompassing, primal fear that overwhelmed him. There was no resisting it. The fear gnawed you until you broke down inevitably, and it consumed your mind.

What if they'd left him there to simply die? He hadn't yet seen an attorney. Nobody would know if they killed him.

Seconds, minutes, hours stretched into infinity, making his torment insufferable.

Stoically, he mustered the last of his resolve, mumbling a prayer. He prayed harder than he ever had before. He had hit the rock bottom of despair, and the only way out of the emotional abyss was up. His fear ebbed away. He steeled himself for whatever lay ahead, knowing that he would get out. Time froze, but hope rekindled.

Creaking, a key turned inside the lock and light spilled inside as the cell opened. Two penal officers manhandled him. Constantine staggered out of the cell and down the corridor to the main block. When they reached another metal door, a third officer shoved a thin mattress to Constantine, which he clutched awkwardly.

A bolt grated and the door screeched open. A shove in the back pushed Constantine inside. Then the steel door slammed shut with finality.

Standing there for a moment, Constantine dropped the mattress to the floor and surveyed his surroundings.

The area was fifteen square meters, give or take. Mold-covered walls with peeling dark-brown paint. A tiny window with iron bars and no frame, allowing sauna-like heat to drift inside. A single ceiling lamp, turned on around the clock. A small fridge in one corner, with an ancient television set on top, always switched on as well. In the other corner, a washbasin and a toilet. Six bunk beds. Four pairs of eyes scrutinizing him.

The air was heavy with cigarette smoke and the stench of humanity.

"What's your name?"

The question came from a short, stocky man in his fifties. His bald head shone with perspiration. His nose was misshapen, broken more than once, and his mouth was full of gold fillings. Because of the heat, he was dressed only in boxer shorts. His thick forearms were overgrown with fuzzy hair. The bare torso displayed a collection of tattoos.

Russian criminals did not ink themselves just for show. Every tattoo relayed coded information, denoting a felon's standing in the underworld and the activities he specialized in, listing his achievements and criminal history, or showcasing his attitude toward the police, the judicial system, and the government in general. Some marks were forced as punishment by fellow inmates who thus branded snitches or rapists. One could learn an entire life story by reading the hidden language of a man's tattoos.

The bald man's fingers were inked with signet rings that comprised a set of pictograms. Constantine wondered what each of those symbols meant, but he knew that together they totaled a high rank. He managed to recognize a few designs on the man's upper body. Eight-pointed stars, shaped like a compass rose, near each shoulder beneath the collarbones signified that the man commanded respect. A pair of eyes tattooed on his chest meant that he was in charge of keeping order among the cell's inmates.

"Constantine Sokolov."

"What're you in for?"

Article 318: Violence against police officers, Constantine didn't say.

Instead, he replied, "Why do you ask?"

The overseer nodded, smiling at the show of character as if Constantine had passed his first test.

"I'm Zachar. You can take that bed over there."

Russian prisons were notoriously overcrowded. It was not uncommon for fifteen or twenty inmates to pack a cell meant for five, like sardines in a can. Constantine was lucky to share the cell with only four others. At least he wouldn't have to wait for his turn in order to get some sleep. He picked up his mattress and chucked it over the bunk bed assigned to him. The bed's placement also carried significance. He'd avoided the one nearest to the toilet, which would have been the ultimate humiliation. The deck was stacked against him, but he could have gotten off to a much worse start.

Zachar turned back to the TV, which showed a report of President Frolov's first few days in office. Even behind bars, there was no escaping the Kremlin propaganda machine.

Constantine couldn't bear to look at the screen, so he sat atop the mattress, stretching his aching limbs, and regarded the other inmates from the corner of his eye.

Remand prisoners were not given orange coveralls or any other uniform, so they all wore their own clothes. The most comfortable, and hence the most widespread in prison, were tracksuits. Apart from Zachar, all three of Constantine's cellmates wore tracksuit bottoms. The youngest one, no more than twenty, had a sleeveless shirt on, and kept to himself, reading a yellowed newspaper. The two others, stripped to the waist, were sitting across from Constantine, playing a game of blackjack. Their bodies were gaunt from a lengthy diet of prison food, but ripped due to workouts and inked all over.

The card dealer was covered with Christian images. In prison tattoos, religious symbology took on an entirely different meaning. A traditional onion-domed cathedral signified conviction, with the number of domes corresponding to prison terms served. Three, in this case. A Madonna with Child alluded to imprisonment since a young age. A crucifix demonstrated allegiance to the gang's moral code.

His buddy had a large swastika on his left biceps. However, it didn't necessarily indicate that he was an avid fan of Adolf Hitler. Nazi symbols stood for contempt for the law. A snarling tiger head was inked on the abdomen as a sign of aggression. Exasperated, he tossed the cards away, flung a towel over his shoulder and headed across the cell toward the basin. Stopping at Constantine's bed, he let the towel slide down and fall to the floor.

"Pick it up."

"It's not mine and I'm not the one who dropped it," Constantine replied coldly.

"I said pick it up, bitch." The swastika-tattooed felon glowered.

Constantine returned his stare. He wouldn't back down. If he showed weakness, he was finished. He was ready to go down fighting, or else he would have stayed in the blackout cell.

The snarling tiger pounced. The felon threw his arm in a well-honed stabbing motion, weapon in hand. He dropped it instantly as Constantine booted him into the groin, the pre-emptive kick connecting with full force in a satisfying smack. Doubling over, the criminal felled next to his weapon. It was a shank made from a sharpened spoon, absolutely deadly in capable hands.

The attacker's church-inked mate sprang to his feet, producing his own shank stashed in his slacks—a row of shaving razors taped to a handle. He swung out at Constantine's jugular.

Before he could slash Constantine's throat, his strike was arrested from behind. Wrestling for the shank, Zachar squeezed his huge paw over the man's hand while using his free arm to constrict the neck in a choke hold. Immensely strong for someone his size, Zachar overpowered him, drawing the shank, still in the man's grip, across his face, disfiguring it. Zachar plowed the razors all the way down the jaw. Blood sprayed from the severed carotid artery. The would-be killer toppled, his tattoos assuming a straightforward context as the last few seconds of his life pumped out.

On the grimy floor, the tiger-tattooed Nazi groped for his spoon shank—but it wasn't there. Zachar was already thrusting it into his flesh. Short, sharp stabs wounded his side, puncturing organs. The tiger was bleeding like a pig before a Sunday roast.

Constantine observed in stunned silence.

Zachar turned to the youngest cellmate. Gaping, he jettisoned his newspaper and rushed to the door. Literally screaming bloody murder, he banged his fists against the stainless steel surface.

The peephole slid open, the locks creaked, the door groaned on its hinges, and the trio of penal officers stormed in from the corridor.

"What's going on here?" the superior officer demanded.

"Nasty business, warden," Zachar answered. "These two good-for-nothing conmen both tried to cheat at cards and ended up cutting each other. See? Nasty business, indeed."

"Sounds a bit too nice and tidy. We'll see about that." Then the officer addressed his men. "Take this newbie away and lock him up in a blackout cell until we're done with this mess."

He was pointing at the young detainee who'd raised the alarm.

"What? Me? I didn't do nothing, chief!" he cried incredulously as they dragged him down the corridor, his voice fading away.

"Help! It's not fair! Let go of me! You sons of ... "

The superior officer muttered to Zachar, "Follow me. *The* man wants to see you."

Zachar nodded to Constantine, and they proceeded out of the cell, marching to a door at the opposite end of the ward. The officer unlocked it and beckoned for them to enter.

"Come on in," Zachar told Constantine.

As Constantine stepped into a Butyrka cell for the second time in a matter of minutes, he couldn't believe his eyes.

15

The cell was Butyrka's royal suite. It could give most Russian hotel rooms a run for their money. There was a single bed, a leather sofa, a dining table with a couple of chairs. Persian tapestry covered the floor and draped the walls. An air conditioning unit chugged steadily, blowing a cool current. Air bubbles streamed in a fish aquarium with live guppies. A row of worn, well-read volumes lined a bookshelf. If not for the lack of windows, Constantine would never have guessed he was still inside the prison.

A man in his late sixties was sitting alone at the table. He wore a gunmetal gray satin shirt underneath a brand new Adidas tracksuit which concealed his expanding waistline. His face was doughy, clean-shaven, with eyes as cold and hard as onyx. Receding charcoal-gray hair was combed back and slick with product. Tattooed on his left wrist was an eagle's head. His fingers, too, were inked with cryptic signet icons.

When he spoke, his voice was quiet but authoritative.

"Do you know who I am?"

Constantine sure did.

"Aram Boghossian."

He was a *vor v zakone*—the highest rank in the Russian underworld, equivalent to the Italian *capo*. And Aram Boghossian was the most infamous mob boss of them all. The scope of his gang's activities reached far beyond Russia. He personified Russian organized crime in the rest of the world. Drug-trafficking, extortion, money-laundering, and fraud charges had put him on the FBI Ten Most Wanted Fugitives list and the top of Interpol's Most Wanted Persons.

"You can call me Uncle Ari. And you, do you have a nickname?"

Constantine shook his head.

"You're a historian, aren't you? Take a seat, Historian. Have some tea."

Constantine pulled a chair under the watchful eye of Boghossian's bodyguard—a hunk wearing a see-through tank top to show off overblown muscles. Zachar stayed behind, also tracking Constantine's every motion as he sat at the table.

Only now did Constantine notice an enormous plastic plate overloaded with appetizers—smoked salmon *blini* pancakes topped with a caviar dressing. Rumbling, his stomach reminded him that he hadn't eaten anything since the McDonald's meal.

"You must be starving."

Constantine made a tough decision.

"Thanks, but no thanks. I'm not hungry. Wouldn't mind the tea, though," he said, pouring himself a cup from a steaming teapot. It tasted better than it actually was.

The crime boss chuckled. "I like you, Historian. Your defiance is a rarity nowadays. You know a little bit about me. I know *everything* about you. You're here because of *him.*" Boghossian gestured at the forty-inch LED TV panel mounted in the corner of the cell, tuned in to the Frolov program. "Our new President ordered to have you killed. No muss, no fuss. The prison authorities made those two half-wits do it for them. So I asked Zachar to intervene."

"Why? Do I owe you something now?"

"Consider it a gesture of good will. You see, I once fought against a rival who wanted to take away my business. A powerful oligarch. Robertas Dedura. Does the name ring a bell?"

"Maybe."

"Anyway, this competitor of mine died under rather mysterious circumstances. I know what really happened to him, Historian. I appreciate what you and your brother did that day. Thanks to you, my profits have soared, especially in Europe. Unfortunately, Dedura had an even more powerful associate. Saveliy Frolov. He locked me up here as soon as he became President. So when you arrived here and I learned about his plans for you, I decided to give you your due and spite him at the same time."

"I'm humbled."

"You and I share a lot in common, more than you might think. I don't have a formal education, but in my lifetime I've spent enough years in prison to read thousands of books. I enjoy history. In 1908, during a more humane era, Harry Houdini performed his famous escape act before a crowd of Butyrka inmates. He was shacked and sealed in an iron box. To the delight of the audience, he emerged free after twenty-eight minutes. Do you think you can pull off a stunt like that?"

"I'm no magician."

"But my attorney is. Mark Goldstein runs the best law firm in Moscow. He's on his way here. You'll be released within twenty-eight minutes of his arrival. But then, it'll mean that I've already done you an extra favor."

Constantine should've guessed that a *vor v zakone* wasn't letting him off the hook so easily.

"If I accepted your generous offer, Uncle Ari, I couldn't possibly repay the debt."

Boghossian's face remained impassive. "I'm aware of the true reason Frolov wants to get rid of you. You've been nosing around too much. Now I'll tell you something about myself. I'm a Yazidi Kurd, but I was born in Armenia. My whole family was killed by the 1988 Armenian earthquake. My parents ... my sisters ... everyone. My hometown of Spitak was destroyed completely."

"I'm sorry. It was a terrible tragedy." Constantine was a kid back then, but he remembered the horrible footage from the disaster area. Along with Chernobyl, the Armenian earthquake summed up the twilight of the Soviet Union in an almost mystical way.

"Yes, it stunned the world. In the aftermath, the U.S. and Europe offered their help immediately, sending in medical supplies, equipment, and personnel. I'll never forget the aid they provided to my people. And there's something else I'll always remember. On the eve of the disaster, I talked on the phone to my father, and he told me that it was coming. The KGB was about to test some sort of weapon that could cause terrifying devastation. I believed him only when fifty thousand died overnight, including himself, and two hundred thousand were injured. Later, I received irrefutable proof that the KGB had waged an act of geophysical war against Armenia. I had eyes and ears everywhere, and I still do. The KGB man who's assumed the Kremlin throne is killing my fellow Kurds in Syria, and he won't stop there. So here's the deal. Promise me one thing, Historian. When you get out, you'll do everything you can to make sure it never happens again."

16

On his way out of the Butyrka, Constantine endured a foul-mouthed tirade from the penal officers as he reclaimed the personal effects—his wristwatch and wallet. It struck him as odd that crime lord Aram Boghossian eschewed obscene language—unlike the jailers and policemen who were supposed to protect the society from the likes of Uncle Ari, but whose mouths were dirtier than toilet bowls. At the top of the criminal hierarchy, any profanity could be taken literally, resulting in bloodshed. Respect was the most prized asset. Russian gangsters lived by a certain code, which couldn't be said of Russian officials. Constantine could hardly draw a line between them, or honestly say which of the two intertwined groups disgusted him more. Against the Kremlin Khan, a *vor v zakone* seemed like the lesser of two evils.

Curiously enough, Butyrka prison was located in downtown Moscow, just four kilometers from Red Square and three from Constantine's apartment. The prison officers had acted like petty thieves. The wallet had been cleaned out of cash, but it still held an unused subway ticket. He walked toward Novoslobodskaya station. His release from jail should have brought him elation, but he felt flat. The streets of Moscow carried no more freedom than the walls of the Butyrka. The people didn't differ much, either. Nobody ever smiled. Throughout his commute, passing by throngs of people, he saw only hostility and fear registered in their gloomy faces and their dead eyes.

He descended underground, the forty-meter-long escalator taking him deep into the chasm of the station, which doubled as a bomb shelter. Instead of going home when he reached Presnya, he took an extra stop and got off at Kievskaya station. He exited the ornate vestibule and headed to the sprawling shopping mall across the street. In the parking lot, he fished out a key fob given to him by Mark Goldstein.

Constantine pressed a button and the saw the blink of hazard lights in the distance. In a row parked cars, a black pearl Jeep Grand Cherokee was waiting as promised.

"You can forget about your brother's Audi," the gray-haired lawyer had told him, eyes grinning wryly behind horn-rimmed glasses as he jotted the address on the back of his business card. "Some crooked cop decided to keep it for himself. It's gone for good. The Jeep will have to make do, courtesy of Uncle Ari. Decent compensation, if you ask me. You'll find everything you need inside."

Constantine climbed in the driver's seat of the old SUV and opened the glove box. Indeed, he discovered a wad of cash and a smartphone. He powered it on and examined the device carefully. It was a cheap, low-end model with a lackluster screen, sluggish interface, and a few scratches collected over months of use. Probably stolen, too.

Despite all the flaws, the phone had a couple of positives going for it.

An Internet connection and a fully functional app store.

17

Berlin. A medieval Slavic town which would thrive with the arrival of German settlers. From the Margraviate of Brandenburg to the Kingdom of Prussia to the Deutsches Reich, it blossomed under the Hohenzollerns. Ravaged by two World Wars, with the rise and fall of the Third Reich in between, Berlin was split between the Allies and the Soviets, like Germany herself. Joseph Stalin, however, hated sharing the spoils. He wanted all of Europe, all of Germany, and all of Berlin. Deep inside the Soviet Occupation Zone of Germany, the American, British, and French sectors were targeted in the first conflict of the Cold War.

On June 24th, 1948, the Soviets cut off all ground access to Western-controlled Berlin, halting traffic, severing the food supply, and shutting off the electricity. The city had to surrender completely or else the entire population of the three Allied sectors was condemned to an excruciating death. Two million civilians, held hostage by Stalin, with no chance of escape.

The Berliners refused to give up. The looting and mass rape carried out by the Red Army was still fresh in their memory.

The Berlin Blockade began.

It would last eleven months. All that time, the Allies delivered supplies to the beleaguered city—by air. It was an unimaginable logistical feat, but it had to be done. President Truman was determined to save Berlin. Failure was not an option.

When the airlift got off to a start, the trickle of incoming cargo grew into a torrent.

The USAF and RAF crews worked tirelessly. Soon they were operating 1,500 flights *per day*. The daily payload increased, averaging 4,000 to 5,000 tons of food and other supplies, well above the minimum required to prevent starvation. Flour and wheat, meat and fish, coffee, sugar, salt, vegetables, powdered milk, and real milk for children. The residents of Berlin no longer had to scour garbage cans or eat grass. But as the blockade dragged on, their lives were still in danger.

The long, freezing winter was approaching. There was a severe shortage of coal to heat the homes and run whatever industry remained. Cut off from energy sources, the city was doomed.

So the Allies started airlifting coal.

In order to allow the increased load, additional airfields had to be constructed. Thousands of Berliners labored around the clock to build the runways by hand.

At the peak of the operation, an Allied plane landed in Berlin every minute, and record tonnage was reached on Easter, 1949, when the aircraft delivered 13,000 tons of supplies in twenty-four hours.

In total, the Berlin Airlift brought in 2.32 million tons of cargo in 278,228 flights. Almost two-thirds of it was coal—a staggering one and a half million tons.

The airlift had a demoralizing effect on the Soviets. Eventually, it was their resolve that was broken. Seeing the futility of the blockade, Stalin capitulated.

The Berlin Blockade ended in a resounding moral victory for the West. The outcome shaped the future landscape of the Cold War. From a military standpoint, it galvanized a stronger relationship between the U.S. and Europe in the face of the Soviet threat. The need for increased U.S. Army presence became apparent, as well as the development of a joint defense strategy. The blockade acted as a catalyst for the formation of NATO.

It also spurred a pivotal reaction, away from the public eye, among the Western elite. The most powerful individuals on both sides of the Atlantic, leaders in politics, industry, and academia, grew increasingly concerned by the challenge posed by communism. They agreed that it was necessary to defend the values of liberty, free market capitalism, and Western civilization as a whole. An international meeting was proposed to exchange ideas and forge cooperation. The idea received support, a list of participants was drawn up, and the first conference was organized weeks later. Due to its sensitive nature, it took place at a private location and the attendees were sworn to maintain confidentiality.

And thus, the Brandenburg Club was born.

18

The clandestine gatherings of the Brandenburg Club were held annually, alternating between European and American venues. The last few meetings had taken place in Virginia, Switzerland, New York, Scotland, Quebec, and Italy. This year's conference marked a return to its roots—West Berlin.

The upper-class borough of Grunewald, a locality famous for the expansive forest of the same name, was a quiet, wealthy area of tree-lined streets and traditional villas. Tucked into the green surroundings were the Rot-Weiss Tennis Club, various foreign embassies, and the five-star Schlosshotel.

The luxury hotel was housed in Palais Pannwitz, built between 1912 and 1914 by Walter von Pannwitz, a renowned art collector and lawyer to Kaiser Wilhelm II, who was the villa's first guest. The extravagant palace had cost an extraordinary ten million Gold Marks, not least due to the lavish use of gold leaf. Von Pannwitz had designed the palace himself to accommodate his art collection. Palais Pannwitz was a work of art in its own right, celebrating the French Baroque with carved wooden walls, soaring ceilings adorned with plaster friezes, silk wallpaper, and a grandiose marble staircase.

Berlin's most magnificent private home had survived two world wars to become the Schlosshotel. Its 54 rooms and suites had been renovated by fashion designer Karl Lagerfeld and now offered modern amenities. The wine cellar had been converted into an underground pool and spa.

The palace was surrounded by its own park-like garden, ensuring extra privacy, making it the perfect setting for the Brandenburg Club meeting.

Discretion was paramount. Twenty-four hours before the guests' arrival, the Schlosshotel employees had been moved out and replaced by the Club's own staff, from chefs and waiters to housekeepers and bell boys. Private security contractors swept every room for bugs and guarded the hotel perimeter, ready to shoot anyone trying to penetrate it. The German government had lent the support of its law enforcement agencies. Plain-clothes BND agents flooded Grunewald. Police checkpoints screened any cars approaching Brahmsstrasse.

Since its beginnings in the 1950s, the Brandenburg Club had morphed into the driving force behind key global affairs. Its members were the real decision-makers who shaped their countries' policies, pulling the strings behind the scenes. The magnitude of its influence had grown, yet the principles of the Brandenburg Club remained unchanged.

The only official position was that of Chairman, currently held by Count Louis de Grenier de Villenueve, CEO of a multinational financial group. The role was largely nominal, drawing upon his organizational skills to prepare each conference, invite guests, and set the agenda. The actual meetings were informal and had no strict procedure. There were no panels or round tables, no records kept. Over two days, the participants engaged in free discussions, expressing different views. The resulting conclusions would later be put into practice around the globe. The only rule forced upon the Brandenburg Club invitees was an oath of silence. An honest exchange of opinions demanded utter secrecy.

Of the Club's three hundred members, a core group which numbered fifty had arrived to the Schlosshotel early on the first day of the conference. The inner circle of the most influential figures who had succeeded the Club's founders.

They assembled in the Spiegelzimmer—a spacious, 70-square-meter meeting room of wall-sized mirrors, wood and gilt, plush sofas and club chairs.

Louis de Grenier, his hairline still strong for a fifty-year-old, kept his body fit and his face suntanned with outdoor sports activities. He wore an ivory long-sleeved mandarin-collar shirt, bespoke black trousers, black leather loafers, and a Chopard Mille Miglia wristwatch.

In his opening note, he welcomed the participants and outlined the agenda. It included one main item: *Russia's attempts to destabilize the West and the counter-measures to fight the Russian aggression.*

To begin with, everyone agreed that the Russian problem had risen to the forefront. A German participant voiced his concern over Russian hackers interfering with elections around Europe. A member from Italy blamed the Kremlin's deliberate actions in the Middle East for the humanitarian crisis and the tide of refugees swarming the continent. According to an American speaker, Western society was suffering from an unprecedented level of division fueled by a stream of fake news originating from Moscow. A Briton advocated stronger sanctions against Frolov who had "quite frankly become a bloody nuisance."

"The Cold War has never ended," said another American. If anyone could make that claim, it was him. Harry Richardson, former U.S. National Security Advisor. A veteran Cold Warrior with a few decades' worth of experience in high-level diplomacy. Some called him the puppet-master of Western politics, a reputation that didn't match his genial, bowtie-wearing appearance.

"The collapse of the USSR was a ruse," he continued. "The Soviet deception strategy of perestroika was described by KGB defector Anatoly Golitsyn back in the 1960's, but many of us turned a blind eye to his warnings. When communism fell, we thought that the job was done. History proved Golitsyn right. Under the guise of democratic transition, the Communist Party transferred its power to the real winner—the KGB. The world's deadliest organization. We'd gone mellow, sitting idly as a resurgent Russia expanded its sphere of influence and regained lost territories. After Georgia, Ukraine, and now Kazakhstan, the reality has become abundantly clear. This corrupt, oppressive, and violent regime cannot coexist peacefully with countries that value liberty, so the Kremlin will export corruption, oppression, and violence to the rest of the world. And it won't stop ... not until the Cold War is finally won. Frolov's Russia presents an existential threat to our civilization."

A Belgian participant voiced his reservations, arguing that with the size of its economy, Russia could not possibly challenge the rest of the world.

"Two percent of the world's GDP may not sound like a lot for a country," Richardson countered. "But for a terrorist group? The Kremlin isn't competing with us in the open marketplace. It's fighting us as enemies. And the regime in Russia has brought all of the nation's wealth under its control. Tell me, who else can attack us using two percent of the global economy?"

"Certainly not the Islamists," added a Canadian. "Besides, the Kremlin has been supporting them for decades."

Reluctantly, the Belgian conceded.

"All viewpoints are welcome, but I'm glad that we have reached a consensus," said the Chairman. "Solidarity among us is vital. The danger we are facing is far greater than cyber-attacks and propaganda. One of our members, Dr. Dmitry L. Ivanov, has prepared a working paper on the issue. As you know, Mr. Ivanov is a Nobel Prize winner and one of the world's leading physicists. He has amassed evidence of the Kremlin's engagement in environmental warfare."

A wave of agitated murmurs rippled across the Spigelzimmer.

De Grenier went on. "Dr. Ivanov will present his report tomorrow and make copies of it available to all Club members. If his accusations are valid, then far more drastic measures against Russia will be required."

They all knew what that meant. They would have to deliver the killer blow.

"But first," Count de Grenier glanced at his Chopard, "let us enjoy a fantastic dinner tonight."

19

The Gulfstream G550 touched down at Schönefeld airport, its sleek white airframe gleaming in the late-afternoon sun. The business jet came to a stop and the main entry door opened. A young woman descended the airstair, wearing a dark Chanel pantsuit, accompanied by an Armani-clad bodyguard who had his hands full with a Louis Vuitton travel bag and carry-on. The whine of Gulfstream's Rolls-Royce engines subsided.

And a Rolls-Royce with an idling BMW engine, a 6.6-liter twin-turbocharged V12, awaited the passengers as they deplaned. The diamond-black Ghost super-luxury sedan was based on the BMW 7-Series, smaller, cozier, and sportier, but with all the class and elegance of the senior Phantom. The chauffeur got out to greet the VIP clients.

"*Willkommen!*"

Tanned face, short-cropped blond hair, black jacket and white shirt concealing muscle and hardware. He was a private security contractor hired by the Brandenburg Club.

He released the trunk with a foot movement, activating the proximity sensor, and helped load the luggage inside.

Then the chauffeur held up his phone, approaching the woman.

"Just a small formality before we can proceed," he explained in clipped English.

Her bodyguard moved forward to shield her.

"It's okay," she said, waving him away.

The bodyguard's square jaw tightened, but he obeyed without a word, stepping aside.

The chauffeur brought the phone camera to her eye level. The iris scan confirmed the woman's identity. Asiyah Kasymova. Satisfied, he nodded, and opened the rear-hinged coach door in a smooth motion.

"You know my name," she said. "What's yours?"

"Hans," the chauffeur replied.

She got into the passenger seat. The bodyguard climbed in front next to Hans.

Shortly, the Ghost was breezing toward Berlin along the A113 autobahn.

Nestled in the creamy leather seat, her feet resting on a lambswool floormat, Asiyah watched the lush green German countryside roll by through the tinted window. Her mind was racing, consumed by a nine-digit figure.

Nine hundred million dollars.

It was the amount of her secret money cache. An emergency fund stashed in a Swiss bank account. There were others, siphoned off government contracts by her late father, the tyrannical President of Kazakhstan, totaling several billion. But the secret Swiss account was registered in her own name, and thus the easiest to access. Only an iris scan was required, not dissimilar to the one performed at the airfield.

Just a hundred mil shy of a billion. So near, and yet so far.

For her, it was a matter of survival. And freedom.

For the past few months, she had lived under FSB protection in Sochi—virtually as a prisoner. She'd bargained for her life, and Frolov had agreed to spare it in exchange for her expertise. A product of her father's Islamist training camp, she had shared her knowledge at a terrorist base in the mountainous area outside Sochi. She had helped train women and young girls who would then travel to Europe through Syria as refugees.

She was too dangerous to Frolov outside his control. Like her father, Frolov had made her complicit in his crimes as a means of protecting himself. He'd given her no other choice. Until now.

"I'm asking you for a favor," he'd told her in the Red Room of the Kremlin. *"An errand which nobody else can run for me. I need you to act as my envoy at the Brandenburg Club meeting. After that, the matter between us will be settled.*

In its attempts to contain China and Iran, the CIA had sought to strengthen ties with Kazakhstan as a key player in the Caspian region. One of the benefits which Timur Kasymov had brokered was Brandenburg Club membership, with his daughter as the obvious choice to represent his interests. She had become the first Asian woman in the exclusive group, eagerly accepted by the politically correct establishment. Frolov was aware of the fact that she had attended the previous Club meeting.

She didn't put much stock in his promise to let her go once she had completed the assignment. He and Timur Kasymov were cut from the same cloth. She was absolutely certain that Frolov would get rid of her once she was no longer useful. Her guard, Grishin, might look clumsy wearing a designer suit on his hulking frame. He cut a different, much more fearsome figure in his military fatigues with gun in hand, she reminded herself. The man was an ice-cold killer from the FSB Alpha special forces team. She'd seen him in action as he led his men into battle, and she knew the brutality he was capable of. Grishin was infinitely loyal to Frolov, who'd instructed him to keep a constant eye on her—and eliminate her if necessary. But she wasn't going to wait like a lamb to the slaughter until that moment arrived. She would seize her chance to break free. Dead or alive, she wouldn't be going back to Russia. A plan was forming in her head.

The Gulfstream had arrived in Berlin via Paris. The reasons for the stopover had been twofold: French lenience over flights originating from Russia, and Asiyah's shopping trip. A lady could only attend a social event in a dress that matched the occasion. Moscow's fashion imports were inadequate for the task, paling in comparison to the glitz of Parisian boutiques. With Grishin trudging in tow, she had scoured every *haute couture* brand store stretching from Avenue Montaigne to Boulevard Haussmann. The spoils of Asiyah's spending spree were packed into the new Louis Vuitton suitcase. At least something good should come out of a Kremlin-bankrolled mission, she mused.

Her reverie was broken as Hans swung the car into an alley, clearing a police roadblock and driving through the massive iron gates of Palais Pannwitz. The Rolls-Royce Ghost came to a halt at the end of the driveway in front of the main entrance.

She admired the serene surroundings, the hotel's vast lobby of red brocatello, the marble staircase, and her deluxe room—vast, sophisticated, styled in black, white, and gold tones.

Grishin dropped the monogrammed bags next to the king bed.

"Get ready for dinner," he told her gruffly. "I'll be waiting outside."

The door slammed shut. Finally alone, Asiyah unzipped the LV carry-on and unpacked its contents—Nike gymwear and her evening dress, which she laid out atop the bed.

She plopped down on a sumptuous armchair and kicked away her high heels. She discovered letter stationery in a desk drawer, and wrote a note for the housekeeping staff, leaving it alongside a generous 100-Euro tip.

Then she padded across the carpeted floor into the bathroom. Hot water gushed into the deep tub as she turned on the faucet.

In front of the mirror, she stripped out of her clothes and gazed at her slender body. She ran her manicured hands over her curves, perfectly shaped through intense fitness workouts. Raven-black hair framed her face, highlighting her delicate features. Her classic feminine beauty required minimal makeup to shine. Physically, she was as stunning as her Russian mother. Asiyah had inherited her gorgeous looks—but not her personality. Deep down inside, she shared her father's temperament. Timur Kasymov had claimed to be a descendant of Genghis Khan, and she saw it now. The reflection showed something in her hazel eyes that no iris scan could ever determine.

The woman in the mirror had the cold stare of a killer.

20

Dinner was served in the Musikzimmer—an 85-square-meter, pistachio-colored ballroom lit by a pair of crystal chandeliers. The wall facing the tall windows was dominated by a pastoral Rococo painting. Across the polished hardwood floor, banquet tables had been arranged in a U-shaped formation to seat the gathering guests.

Asiyah was sat next to a U.S. Senator whose family had played a significant role in American politics spanning over one hundred years and four generations. He complimented her cocktail dress, a Saint Laurent of black silk with a metallic polka dot design and a swooping neckline. Her tiny shoulder bag of black leather matched it perfectly.

Asiyah scanned the Musikzimmer. She picked out Count de Grenier and Harry Richardson, as well as a few other familiar faces, but Dmitry Ivanov was nowhere to be seen.

Over hors d'oeuvres, the room became filled with the sounds of clinking cutlery and soft conversation.

"I was sad to hear about your father's death," Senator Fairchild said, digging into a duck foie terrine.

"Thank you. It's a difficult time for myself and my country."

"What's going on in Kazakhstan? Are the Russians marching in?"

"The government is in turmoil. There is a chance of a pro-Russian candidate winning the elections. But whatever plans the Kremlin had regarding Kazakhstan have been put on the back-burner against Russia's bigger problems."

"Yeah, Frolov is one unpredictable bastard. What do you think about tomorrow's report? There's so much buzz around it."

"Let's wait and see," Asiyah said. "But I'm not getting my hopes up."

Finally, she spotted her target. Nobel Prize winner Dmitry L. Ivanov had quietly taken his designated seat next to Richardson. They were exchanging a few words and some laughs as he apologized for his late arrival.

Dr. Ivanov sported a three-piece suit and a goatee as white as his curly hair. He was going strong both physically and mentally despite his age. He still taught at Stanford, where Asiyah had taken his class. His eyes were as lucid as ever, despite the scars his mind and body had endured at the hands of Andropov's KGB. Today, he remained an outspoken critic of Andropov's successor, President Saveliy Frolov.

The main course followed. Asiyah had opted for Dover sole with Gilardeau oyster and black truffle. Senator Fairchild was working on a veal sirloin. An incident broke out from their cultural difference. In accordance with European utensil etiquette, Asiyah held the fork in her left hand as she ate, while Fairchild switched the knife and fork back and forth into his right hand, American style. Inevitably, Asiyah's elbow bumped into the Senator's arm, perhaps with a little too much force, and the steak knife tumbled to the floor. She gasped, terribly sorry, and he grinned sheepishly, the fault all his. A waiter quickly fetched a replacement to end the awkward moment.

She continued watching Ivanov. As the dinner drew to a close, the Russian rose from the table exited the Musikzimmer into the garden. Asiyah excused herself and followed Ivanov outside. The evening air felt cool and fresh before sunset. The light was fading, not so much from advancing nightfall, but due to the storm clouds forming in the distance. She joined him as he stood there, gazing into the sky hued with violet and rose-pink.

"Something's wrong," he muttered to himself. "This cloud formation is abnormal."

"Good evening, Dr. Ivanov."

He swung around, startled by her presence. His eyes flashed recognition.

"Oh! Good evening ... Asiyah? My word, you've blossomed into a real beauty."

"Why, thanks for the compliment. It's been a few years. I'm glad you remember me at all."

"Believe me, you're not easy to forget for any man. What can I do for such a remarkable young lady?"

"I'm sure you'll find it much easier to accept my offer."

From her shoulder bag, she produced a micro memory card and handed it to Ivanov.

"What is this?" he inquired, looking at it quizzically as he held it.

"It's an updated version of your report," she said coldly. "You will present it tomorrow before the Brandenburg Club members. As we both know, even the best research is hardly ever definitive. You'll say that there is no conclusive proof of Russia's involvement in weather manipulation. There are some alarming signals that need to be worked on, but only together. All countries should join forces to battle climate change. Russia should be viewed as a key partner, not an adversary, if we want to save the planet."

Ivanov's face grew crimson, then purple, as if he were about to have a stroke. His whole body shook with rage.

"You're working for him! For them. The KGB!" he panted.

"The KGB is long gone. You should reevaluate your position. In exchange, you will receive unlimited resources and the ability to continue the development of Mercury-18. You'll never get another opportunity like this in your lifetime."

"How dare you? How *dare* you presume that I would accept such a despicable offer!"

"I'm just the messenger."

He flung the memory card into the grass.

"I'll take that as a no, then," she said calmly and walked away, crossing the garden.

Her mission had come down to only one objective: convincing Ivanov to switch sides.

She'd failed.

Grishin was watching from the shadows. No doubt, he'd witnessed the encounter and Ivanov's refusal to cooperate. The FSB man would have to do something about it. Her failure wouldn't go unpunished.

The less than subtle approach had been intentional. Deep down, she resented working for Frolov. While she couldn't openly defy Frolov, she let the professor do it for her. It was part of her plan. She'd calculated the risk of the consequences she was about to face.

She didn't know what Grishin's reaction would be. But the steak knife hidden inside her bag gave her more confidence about her chances of survival. And freedom.

21

The athletic man in plaid shirt and faded Levi's roamed the streets of Grunewald on two wheels, a backpack strapped to his shoulders. Driving by, he saw that Brahmsstrasse was sealed off by a police cordon—a blue-and-white Opel cruiser and a couple of uniformed officers on the watch. He didn't linger long enough to get noticed by them or any undercover policemen who might be around, even though the visor concealed his face. He was riding a Vespa GTS Super 300 scooter. At first glance, it hardly resembled the iron horse befitting a Cossack, but the scooter packed some serious punch, capable of hitting a top speed of 122 km/h thanks to its 278cc engine. Eugene Sokolov pressed the throttle and the nimble Vespa zipped along Richard-Strauss-Strasse.

Colonel Lisovsky's laptop had turned out to be a treasure trove of intel. Using a trick he'd learned from a former tech wiz friend, Sokolov had bypassed the computer's password protection by entering recovery mode. From there, he'd been able to access every file in storage. He'd spent the better part of his flight to Berlin reading classified GRU documents. He'd found out that Lisovsky had been a high-level officer running Russian covert activities in Europe. He'd also uncovered the target of the mission involving Asiyah, and the venue. The Brandenburg Club meeting at Palais Pannwitz.

Asiyah had already arrived there by the time of his plane's touchdown at Schönefeld, so he was playing catch-up.

A soft probe of Grunewald required stealth and mobility. During the S-Bahn trip from the airport to the city, he'd browsed the local marketplace listings and found the online ad for the Vespa. The seller—a man inked with more tattoos than a rock singer—had been offering the Vespa in mint condition for a fraction of its real value, helmet included. The catch? He'd had no registration papers for the scooter, claiming that he'd lost them. Just the keys for cash. They'd made the exchange outside Berlin Central Station. No paperwork, no ID, no trail. Whether the man had been the actual owner or a bike thief was a whole different story. Sokolov didn't mull over it. But he knew for a fact that the Vespa was a popular choice among street criminals.

He, too, appreciated its maneuverability as he scouted the area around the Schlosshotel.

The hotel premises were off limits behind heavy security. Asiyah was unreachable—*if* she was there. He couldn't be one hundred percent certain without visual contact.

He had no other leads to follow. His best bet now was to watch and wait. He wouldn't fail to identify her on the way *out* of the hotel.

Finding a suitable stake-out position proved to be a challenge. The rows of detached houses were inaccessible, and, shielded by trees, none offered a decent view of the street anyway. He couldn't spend too much time scouting the surroundings, though. Beneath Grunewald's pleasant appearance, the neighborhood was tight security-wise. It was a fancy district of homeowners, car owners, and dog owners. Any outsider cruising around would stick out like a sore thumb, even on a scooter. The residents wouldn't hesitate to call the police.

He picked out a spot further down Richard-Strauss-Strasse. He came across a tall three-story edifice which belonged to a dermatology clinic. Its rooftop jutted above the dense foliage, facing Palais Pannwitz directly across the street.

He only had to figure out how to get in. It was late, well past the private clinic's business hours. The gate, topped by a pair of cherub statues, was locked.

He parked the scooter curbside, shut down the engine and took off his helmet. Then he approached the aluminum fence and tossed the helmet over the side. No alarm sounded when he heard it hit the ground. So far, so good. He scaled the fence and leaped down, landing on his feet. He picked up the helmet, attached it to the strap on the backpack, and went to the back of the house. Using the fire escape, he climbed to the roof. Next to the slanting attic, it had a flat section where Sokolov set up shop.

Peering through the binoculars, he had to give credit to the Brandenburgers. They couldn't have chosen a better location for the conference. The treetops obstructed the line of sight even from his vantage point, perched on the highest building in the area. Only the red roof tiles of Palais Pannwitz were visible. Whatever went on inside remained completely hidden. He had a clear view of Brahmsstrasse, however, so he concentrated on the surrounding activity. It was a mundane task but Sokolov was up for it. If necessary, he could spend hours lying prone on the rooftop. His backpack was stocked with enough supplies to last for a few days. The deteriorating weather was his only concern. Ominous gray clouds were rolling across the sky, pushed by an increasing wind. If it came to worst, the nylon sleeping bag was supposed to be waterproof.

He had to address a far more pressing issue while he waited. He pulled out the laptop and woke it from sleep mode. It connected to a wireless data network, and he logged into his anonymous messenger account. He'd already messaged Constantine back on the train to let him know that he was alive. He checked the inbox again. Still no reply. It was not usual for his brother to go offline for several hours, but this time his gut feeling told him that something damned serious must have happened to Constantine after the crooked policemen had stopped their car.

He was about to contact Klimov, tell him about Constantine's detainment, and ask him for help.

He never did.

Suddenly, a chat bubble popped up.

Constantine: I'm OK. Call me.

His joy quickly evaporated, replaced by apprehension.

What if the message was fake? The FSB might have hacked the account or forced Constantine to send it under duress.

There was only one way to find out.

He tapped the video call button.

Only when he saw his brother's face did he let out a sign of relief.

"Gene! Thank God! Are you all right?"

"Still in one piece. You?"

The poor lighting made it impossible to make out any background detail.

"I'm fine. Don't worry. I'm at a friend's place."

"You've made lots of new friends recently."

"It's a long story. Where are you?"

"I've traced Asiyah to Berlin."

"Berlin? Hmmm. What about those goons you had on your back?"

"Not far away. And you were right, they're planning something big. I need your help."

"Do you want me to make a reservation with Hilton?"

"That'd be great. I've tried to check-in at the Schlosshotel, but it's fully booked. I'd appreciate a room where I could get some rest and drop off the stuff I've picked up along the way. Some of it makes for interesting reading."

A diesel engine roared in the street below. Then came the jarring crash of metal as a pickup truck smashed into the Opel. Muzzle flashes erupted from the truck's cabin, shattering the silence of Grunewald with a chatter of shots. The *Polizei* officers were chopped down before they could react.

"Gene? What's going on over there?"

Another burst of automatic fire finished off the downed policemen, their blood splattering on the Brahmsstrasse pavement.

"It's a terrorist attack," he said soberly. "They're here."

22

At the wheel of the Toyota pickup, Vlad Panin felt a jolt of adrenaline together with the impact of the truck battering the police car. As the two policemen standing next to it scrambled clear of danger, he unleashed a full magazine through the open window, testing the AK on live targets. With desired effect, it ripped holes through *Polizei* flesh. The narcotic effect of a fresh kill washed away Panin's fatigue. He'd come to the end of a seven-hour haul from Serbia, first crossing the Bulgarian border, then flying a chartered plane to Leipzig, and finally driving to Berlin until he reached Grunewald. All he had to do now was cross the finish line: the threshold of Palais Pannwitz. With renewed energy, he yanked the wheel and stomped the accelerator, powering his way through. The truck rammed the iron gate.

The second vehicle, a fake DHL delivery van, followed close behind. Umar directed it in front of the Toyota and braked sharply.

The van's doors burst open and a group of masked, AK-wielding men rushed out.

There were eight of them and they were chomping at the bit, desperate to shed the blood of the infidels. All eight were immigrants from Central Asia, sleeper cell members of the Islamic Levant, a terrorist organization created by the GRU. In Leipzig, Panin had delivered the weapons and picked the best fighters.

Alerted by the gunshots in the street, a trio of dark-suited guards faced the intruders, weapons drawn and firing.

One of the jihadis went down, spewing blood from the hole in his throat, a terrible gurgling noise drowning out his *Al-lahu-akbar!* in mid-cry.

Panin didn't give a damn. They were expendable. Some would die clashing with the main protective detail inside the hotel. He'd rather they got the bullets instead of him.

The three security operators took cover behind the massive stone pillars that supported the balcony above the main entrance. Outgunned, they popped off shots from their semiautomatics and a single FN P90 compact submachine gun. It was enough to deal with a mob of protesters or a lone madman. Against a full-blown military assault, the sheer firepower overwhelmed them.

The jihadis unleashed 40mm frag grenades from the launchers attached under the barrels of their AKs. The projectiles blew up in clouds of smoke and dust, pockmarking the stone façade and disintegrating glass in the tall window panes. Screams echoed the thunderous explosions as fragments sizzled through flesh. A fusillade of slugs tearing into their bodies killed the security men off.

Umar led the charge into the building.

Panin smiled. So far, everything was going as planned. The surprise attack had breached the Brandenburg defense, allowing the jihadis to break in.

Umar was shouting commands as the swarm of Islamic fighters invaded the hotel lobby. Inside, screams mixed with blasting gunfire as they met another wave of security operators.

Now, maximum damage had to be inflicted before the security force could regroup. In the raging chaos and confusion, Panin had other business to attend to. He put on a full-face mask respirator, got out of the Toyota, and circled the hotel building.

The terrorist attack merely served as a distraction.

23

The Brandenburg big shots were enjoying after-dinner drinks in the Cigar Lounge, relaxing on Chesterfield sofas of brown leather. The aroma of quality Cuban tobacco filled the air, carrying faint notes of flowers and manure. Harry Richardson sat puffing on a Cohiba while Count de Grenier was nursing a cognac. Senator Fairchild joined them with a tumbler of Scotch on the rocks.

"I've had a most unfortunate conversation with one of our Club members," Dmitry Ivanov was saying. "She approached me with an outrageous offer to falsify the results of my report in Russia's favor."

"Are you talking about Asiyah Kasymova, by any chance?" asked the Senator.

"It doesn't matter," Richardson said, blowing wisps of smoke and rolling the tip of the cigar on the edge of the ashtray. "Don't get me wrong, your research is ground-breaking. You showcase the level of Russian weather-manipulation efforts in astounding detail. But it's just another red line the Russians have crossed. Your report is just the icing on the cake. There is enough incriminating evidence against Russia's misdeeds that nothing could tip the scale in Frolov's favor. The decision has already been made. No disrespect, but your findings merely reaffirm it. Brilliantly, I might add. Our Club members will see that for themselves tomorrow."

"Thank you," Ivanov said with a hint of a Soviet accent, which he struggled to shake off even after decades of life in America. "So, are you implying that I should've taken the money?"

A few soft chuckles sounded.

"What course of action against Russia do you advocate?" Senator Fairchild inquired.

"Full-blown sanctions coupled with covert activities. No more half-measures," Richardson said. "Hit the Russians where it hurts and hit 'em hard. Beat them at their own game. Turn their biggest weapons against them. Energy, finance, cyber warfare. Ban all imports of crude oil and natural gas from Russia. Seize the dirty money stashed by Kremlin officials in Western banks. Retaliate with cyber-attacks to cripple the Russian infrastructure."

"Now that's a plan I can get behind," the Senator said.

Count de Grenier nodded. "As Chairman, I can attest that a lot of our members share your enthusiasm. They will support this new policy in their respective countries. The three-pronged strike will force Frolov to back down. Otherwise, his regime will crumble in a matter of months, if not weeks."

He was cut off by a cacophony of sharp, rattling cracks echoing from outside.

"What's all that racket?" Fairchild growled. "Fireworks?"

"Some folks must still be celebrating the Fourth of July."

"No, it's something else," Ivanov said. "Gunshots."

Then they heard the screaming.

It pierced the terrified silence that fell in the room.

The sounds of shooting intensified, resonating from the lobby of red brocatello. Only an ornate double door separated it from the Cigar Lounge.

At the other end of the room, the head of Brandenburg security burst in through the Spiegelzimmer entrance. Two ex-SEALs accompanied him, their odd-shaped machine pistols ready for action.

"We're under attack!" he announced, pressing a finger to his earpiece. "You must evacuate immediately. Stay calm and follow me, please."

Splinters flew as a volley stitched a row of bullet holes in the double door, adding extra urgency to his words. The attackers might break in at any moment.

The screams in the lobby died down.

Consumed by panic, Ivanov bolted toward the Spiegelzimmer, ignoring the others as they were shepherded by the security men away from danger.

He didn't make it too far ahead of them.

The window next to the marble fireplace smashed into shards as a metallic object sailed through the air. It landed on the polished wooden floor with a clunk and spewed fumes which contained particles of tear gas and smelled nothing like a Cuban cigar. Then the pyrotechnic device exploded.

The detonation knocked Ivanov off his feet. As it went off, the stun grenade blinded him with an eye-searing flash, burning at a luminous intensity of a few million candela. Apart from disrupting his balance, the deafening 170-decibel roar also caused temporary hearing loss. He lay on the floor for thirty seconds, his senses disoriented. Then, overcoming the throbbing in his head, he opened his eyes to take in the scene of sheer horror that unfolded around him in a blur.

It was carnage.

Automatic fire shredded the leather upholstery of the sofas and the slumped form of Harry Richardson. Next to him, the former Navy SEAL collapsed, shot through the forehead.

Senator Fairchild's corpse lay in a pool of gore, his face unrecognizable.

Count de Grenier's bloodied body sagged against the wall, riddled with bullets.

Crimson rivulets smeared the prone figures of the other security guard and his boss. Looming over them, two gunmen wearing camo suits and full-face respirators finished them off from fire-spitting Kalashnikovs.

Through the haze of cigar smoke and tear gas, it all seemed like a nightmare that was impossible to wake up from.

The killers turned to Ivanov.

Ivanov was screaming at the top of his lungs, hearing no sound. He tried to pick himself up from the floor, but dizziness got the better of him.

The barrel of an AK pointed at him. Tears ran down his face, either from the gas or the raw fear that churned in the pit of his stomach.

He hadn't expected to die today. And yet there he was, a finger twitch away from the rifle belching brain-splattering death. What a waste that would be, he mused. His mind probably held the key to the fate of the entire world.

Do you even know who I am? he wondered, perhaps aloud.

They did. They most certainly did.

The realization petrified him. He suddenly found death more appealing than the possible alternative.

A nylon hood was pulled over his head and secured around his throat. Plastic cuffs locked around his wrists and ankles.

Then the terrorists half-dragged him across the blood-slicked floor.

24

Asiyah shed her dress in the locker room of the deserted spa and gym. She pulled on the Nike sports bra, leggings, sneakers, and zip hoodie, left there by the hotel staff as per her request in the thank you note. She slipped the Saint Laurent handbag—which held the Serbian passport and some cash—over her shoulder and retraced her steps.

She emerged into the cavernous indoor pool area. Light shimmered on the white-painted walls, reflecting off the cobalt-blue water surface. Columns surrounding the enormous swimming pool gave it the appearance of ancient Roman baths. She was heading back toward the garden entrance when sharp pain stabbed her scalp. Someone had grabbed her hair from behind and yanked her head back violently. She cried out. An arm wrapped around her neck in a head lock.

"Where do you think you're going?"

Grishin. She sensed his foul breath as he brought his face to her ear.

"Looking for Hans? He's dead. Your plan was too obvious."

The choke hold tightened, constricting her windpipe.

"Let go," she gasped, digging her fingers into his forearm. It was useless.

"You really thought we'd trust you to handle Ivanov, huh? How stupid. Don't worry, your real job is quite simple. All you have to do is die."

He applied more force, like a python crushing its prey. Her vision began to fade.

With shaking fingers, she unclasped her dangling handbag and groped for the steak knife. Seizing the handle, she thrust the blade up and sliced the wrist that was strangling her. The serrated edge carved flesh open, cutting through tendons and arteries. The excruciating damage forced Grishin to ease his death grip. Instantly, she wriggled free, spun around, and slashed the knife again at Grishin. The blade struck his carotid artery. Blood squirted. With seconds to live, Grishin's eyes widened, his good hand clawing at the gun in his belt holster. Asiyah planted the sole of her sneaker into his abdomen, pushing him away. Grishin staggered back and splashed into the pool. Red mist diffused in the water around him as his body floated like a piece of debris.

Panting after her near-asphyxiation, she tossed the knife into the pool and lurched toward the garden exit.

Her head reeled. The getaway plan was going up in smoke. The walls of the converted wine cellar dampened all sound coming from outside. She'd heard some muffled pops, but she had no idea what was happening there. Was the hotel under assault? No matter. Dazed, she knew one thing for sure. She had to flee, with or without Hans and his Rolls-Royce. She would improvise. Her combat training and survival instinct had served her well thus far.

She reached the top of the stairs leading into the garden and froze in her tracks. It was as far as she got before an AK muzzle jabbed into her ribs.

She turned to her right, in the direction of the terrorist holding her at gunpoint. The crazed stare of his deep-set eyes and the bloodstains on his shoes told her enough. He wouldn't think twice about pulling the trigger.

"Wait ... " she said, stalling. "I'm on your side—"

From her left, a second terrorist approached, telling his comrade to hurry. The first jihadi nodded. He shoved her away, striking her spine with the stock of his rifle, knocking her down. She collapsed on the green grass of the well-kept lawn.

Everything would be over now. How stupid, indeed.

She braced herself for the inevitable, praying that her suffering would end quickly.

The two terrorists became agitated, yelling in a heated exchange. She could hardly grasp their dialect, but they weren't debating her fate. They ignored her altogether, switching their attention elsewhere.

The growing sound of an engine. Not a helicopter, but a high-pitched whine.

She raised her head to witness a scooter charging across the garden, coming right at her.

She couldn't see the man's face behind the visor of his helmet. Her gaze focused on an AK in his grip, blasting away. He sent the scooter drifting on the turf as he fired one-handed, kicking up dirt from the rear wheel and delivering doom from the weapon. He unleashed twin salvos and the terrorists toppled on either side of Asiyah, reduced to lead-riddled cadavers in the blink of an eye.

She sprang to her feet.

The scooter braked and the man called out to her over the idle rattle of the engine.

"Asiyah! Come on!"

He motioned at the pillion seat.

She needed no further invitation. Darting to the scooter, she swung her leg over and mounted behind him.

"Hold on tight!" he told her.

She did. She held onto him like never before.

The reflective visor was hiding his face, but she knew his voice. The deep baritone crying out her name, haunting her ever since the Kremlin banquet when she'd last seen Eugene Sokolov.

25

With Asiyah riding pillion, her arms wrapped around his waist, Sokolov twisted the throttle. The Vespa buzzed, racing back across the 3,000-square-meter garden, along the walkway leading past century-old trees to the main gate of Palais Pannwitz.

Up ahead, Sokolov saw Panin and Umar.

They heaved a well-dressed man through side cargo door of the phony DHL van. The captive slammed against the floor, his hands and feet tied, a hood over his head.

So, this is what it's all about.

Closing in on them, Sokolov aimed the assault rifle which he'd retrieved from a dead jihadi. The AK-47, a.k.a. *Sturmgewehr 44*, originally developed by Hugo Schmeisser. Many decades later, it still ranked as one of the world's finest weapons. A triumph of German engineering over Soviet manufacturing.

He shot at the van's wheels—and missed. The volley hit the battered Toyota pickup as the van drove past it, backing out onto Brahmsstrasse.

Asiyah tugged at his arm. Sokolov swerved sharply just as slugs tore the ground in front of the scooter.

Another jihadi was shooting from a second-floor window. Before he could fire again, Sokolov brought the scooter to a skidding stop and took him out with a precise burst. The terrorist plunged lifelessly to the earth below, head first.

If Asiyah hadn't spotted the shooter, they'd both be dead now.

Clearing the gate, Umar threw the DHL vehicle into a turn, shifted gears, and sped down the street, out of sight.

Sokolov tapped the trigger but the AK's magazine was empty.

Sokolov's training and instinct decided his next move. He followed the van out of the Schlosshotel grounds and turned away from it, whooshing through Brahmsstrasse in the opposite direction.

Chasing the DHL van down would turn his improvised rescue operation into a suicide mission. Neither could he afford to get caught by the BFE+ Bundespolizei counter-terrorism unit. He *had* to flee from Palais Pannwitz before the police—or more terrorists—showed up. He needed to get Asiyah out of there safely, above all else.

Bitter memories of the school siege in Beslan flashed in his mind. Over 1,100 people taken hostage by terrorists. At least 333 dead, mostly children, after Russian federal forces had ended a three-day standoff, attacking with heavy weapons. Tanks and incendiary rockets. Himself, a young EMERCOM operator, caught in the crossfire. Bullets whistling as he escaped from the burning building, the hot lead going through his body and killing the schoolgirl in his arms.

Since he'd first laid eyes on her, Asiyah had reminded him of the one he'd failed to save. He'd vowed that it wouldn't happen again.

As she clung onto him in her embrace, he'd never let her take the bullet meant for him, no matter what.

No doubt, she wasn't the innocent girl his mind wanted him to see in her. But her dark side attracted him stronger than the fantasy image ever had.

Sokolov's extraordinary sense of hearing picked up a sound rolling from the skies, growing in intensity. It wasn't thunder—not yet. He recognized the thumping of Eurocopter rotor blades. A royal-blue Bundespolizei Super Puma helicopter swooped down, circling over Grunewald.

26

Constantine knew that each passing second could spell death to his brother. He tried calling him again, but Gene had gone offline.

He voice-dialed Magda.

"Tell your source that I'm in. Something big has come up and I need to pass it on to him. It's extremely sensitive—and urgent."

"Wait," she exclaimed. "Do you remember the place where we last met? I'm ten minutes away."

"I'll see you there in nine."

He'd get there in seven minutes.

He had to.

He grabbed the Jeep key fob off the table, alongside another souvenir from Uncle Ari, a TT semiautomatic. He tucked it under his belt as he was rushing out the door.

Midnight was fast approaching. Purple hues touched the sky as the sun defected to the West.

Moscow was one of Europe's largest metropolitan areas, but the city's downtown lay within a five-kilometer radius around the Kremlin, bound by the Garden Ring road. In moderate, late-night traffic, any two points inside the circle, such as Neskuchny Garden and Constantine's hideout, were accessible in twenty minutes—if one followed the speed limits. Constantine didn't. He stamped his foot on the accelerator. The speedometer hovered around the 120 km/h mark. Driving one of Uncle Ari's cars, he didn't care about the speed cameras. Even behind bars, a *vor v zakone* stood above the law and instilled fear. Custom number plates, such as those gracing the Grand Cherokee, would be flagged as untouchable to street-level cops.

He flew down Leninsky Prospekt and parked the SUV on the curb of the wide avenue, next to the Neskuchny Garden entrance. He shut down the engine and jumped out, heading across the scenic landscape toward the rotunda.

He checked the phone. Six minutes gone. No new messages.

The bulky firearm dug into his waist beneath the loose shirt. The gun was heavy with history, which seemed to add to its weight. The TT was a legendary model, launched in 1934, with over two million units produced in twenty years. The weapon of choice for Stalin's NKVD goons, still used today by their North Korean counterparts, the 7.62mm pistol had reached peak popularity in the post-Soviet era for its sheer stopping power and virtual untraceability. Thousands of unaccounted TT handguns had flooded the Russian cities, becoming the trademark tool of organized crime. He wondered how many people had been killed from that particular piece.

He observed the lamp-lit rotunda from behind a row of linden trees.

A few agonizing minutes later, she appeared in view.

Magda was walking briskly along a pathway, her features tense. Even in the dim illumination, her stunning beauty glowed. Constantine stood there for a moment, mesmerized by her figure dressed in wispy silk.

Two long shadows trailed her. A couple of brawny thugs, maintaining distance, ten meters behind her. Their glum faces showed aggression and not much intellect. The stockier buffoon, scalp shaved above his narrow forehead, kept his hands in the pockets of his tracksuit. His companion, dressed in similar sportswear, wore a flat cap and carried a paper liquor bag. Both pairs of deep-set eyes were boring into Magda, who seemed unaware of the tail.

She stopped in front of the rotunda. The thugs were closing in on her. Now only a few paces away.

Constantine's intuition spiked into overdrive. He broke cover from beyond the trees, right arm behind his back, fingers wrapped around the TT handle.

"Watch out!" he shouted to Magda.

She turned around, startled.

The shaved-head thug pulled out a switchblade and lunged at her.

Constantine whipped out the gun, racked the slide, and fired. He went for center mass. The TT cracked, thundered. The shot found its mark, and the ruffian collapsed, incapacitated, dropping the knife to the ground.

Instead of breaking off in panicked flight, the second goon discarded the paper bag to reveal a pistol with a suppressor attached to its muzzle. Before he could use it to amend the foiled plan, the TT bellowed again. The slug hit him square in the chest.

Magda sprang away from the two bodies and latched onto Constantine's shoulder, pressing against him instinctively. Realizing what had happened, she looked at her wounded attackers and then at Constantine.

Surprisingly, her voice was as cool as a glacier.

"Thanks for saving my life. Journalism is a dangerous profession in Russia, I've been told. And so is history. Is that why you bring a gun to a date?"

She had quite some nerve. Apart from her initial reaction, she appeared unfazed, whatever torrent of emotions she was feeling inside. Constantine's own pulse was throbbing in his temples. His inner voice told him that journalism was just a part of Magda's qualifications.

"Let's get out of here," he said, "before their back-ups show up."

He took her hand, leading her away from the rotunda.

"Who *are* these men?" she asked, high heels clicking as she tried to keep up with his long strides. "I mean, one of them had a silencer!"

"They're no ordinary punks, that's for sure. Someone sent over to make us look like victims of a mugging gone wrong. Come on, we have to hurry. I must contact Hilton."

"We have to get to my car," she said.

"Forget your car."

"You don't understand. Stephen's there."

Constantine halted.

"Damn."

Another silhouette emerged from the darkness and Constantine aimed his gun.

It was Hilton.

"Hold your horses!" the American said, raising his open palms.

Constantine let out a sigh and put the semiautomatic away.

"I heard a gun go off," the CIA man continued. "What's going on?"

"You and Magda have been followed on your way here," Constantine said. "You can't go back. I'll give you a ride."

The fact that Magda and Hilton had arrived together so quickly and at such a late hour suggested that their relationship wasn't entirely professional. Or else her work in Moscow was not limited to news reporting. Constantine cast the thought aside. It hardly mattered at the moment.

In the twilight, he guided them out of Neskuchny Garden to the Grand Cherokee. Once they climbed inside, Constantine drove toward the Garden Ring beltway.

"There was a terrorist attack in Berlin minutes ago," he explained.

"That's impossible," Magda said. "Every news feed would have exploded with the headline by now."

"It was at Palais Pannwitz, Grunewald."

"My God, no," Stephen muttered. "Oh, no."

"What does that mean?" Magda asked.

"The Brandenburg Club meeting," said Stephen Hilton the Third.

"So it *is* real," Magda said. "The Brandenburg Club is real?"

"It is," Hilton confirmed.

"Or *was*," Constantine corrected. "It might be history."

"How did you learn about the attack?" Hilton inquired.

"My brother witnessed it first-hand. In fact, I heard the first shots over the phone when I talked to him."

"Your brother—Eugene, right? Where is he now?"

"I don't know. The call broke off. But he's somewhere in Berlin. And so is Asiyah Kasymova—if she's still alive. Apparently, she was at the Brandenburg meeting. Gene tracked her down. And he also seized a data drive for your techies to go through. I'm sure you'll find it valuable."

The CIA man furrowed his brow and said, "So what am I supposed to do? You want money for it?"

"No, I want something else. I want you to find Gene and bring him back."

"You *what*?"

"You heard me, Hilton. *Now*. You'll do it right now."

Hilton stared. "You're crazy. Like every Russian."

"I'm a Cossack. And I have a gun."

"You don't understand, Constantine. There's no way I can really help you."

"What do you mean you can't help? You've got the weight of the U.S. Government behind you. We're in this mess because of you. Call in the cavalry."

"I can't just send a cable to the CIA station chief in Berlin and tell him to stick his neck out, for goodness' sakes! There's too much red tape, even in the intelligence community. Rules and protocols must be followed, like it or not, especially when it comes to dealing with terrorism suspects. Your brother would have to be handed over to the German authorities. We don't want to screw with our allies, not on their turf. Besides, I can't act through official Agency channels."

"What the hell are you on about?"

Hilton cleared his throat. "You see, the current administration's stance on Russia has caused a rift inside the intel community. Some believe it's too lenient. I belong to a group that views the Kremlin as America's number one enemy—a splinter group, I regret to say. And given the extreme sensitivity of the Mercury-18 affair, only a handful of people inside that group know about it. True patriots. Harry Richardson was one of them. He was the main man, the driving force behind our efforts to stop Frolov. But it was very much informal."

"Cut the crap."

"I'm not bullshitting you. I've been acting without Langley's approval. Your brother is on his own now. I'm sorry."

Constantine's heart sank.

"You're a bastard, Hilton."

His fingers clenched around the steering wheel, anger and desperation welling up.

After a long silence that filled the car, a wild thought occurred to him. It was a long shot.

When he spied the red-lit *M* symbol of the nearest subway station, he pulled the car over.

"Out, Hilton."

"What?"

"I'm sorry. You're on your own now."

Wordlessly, the CIA man got out of the car. No sooner had the passenger door snapped shut than Constantine pulled away from the curb, leaving the American behind, his figure receding in the rearview mirror.

"What about you, Magda?" Constantine asked.

"You want me to get out at the next bus stop?" she asked sardonically.

"Not really. Do you have any contacts in Germany? Someone you can trust?"

"I do. A man named Simon Werner. He has my full confidence," Magda said without hesitation.

"Who is he?"

"A fellow journalist. We met during a trip to the Donbass warzone. He warned me about an upcoming Russian offensive. That got me out of the way of artillery fire. He probably saved my life."

So that's where the ice-cold streak in her character had come from. She'd witnessed far worse than a few street punks getting their due.

He outlined his plan to her.

When he finished, Magda said, "You *are* crazy. Stephen will be fuming when he hears it."

"He has no say in the matter. Gene and I have put our lives on the line get this intel. It doesn't belong to Hilton or the U.S. Government. I can use it as I see fit, and share it with anyone I choose, especially with my brother's life hanging in the balance."

"I see your point. And Stephen will, too, eventually. You need him for your plan to work, you know."

"I know. But from now on, he'll be playing by my rules."

"I'll try to convince Stephen to play along. He has the clout to charter a flight out of Moscow on short notice. For my part, I'll do my best."

"You're an angel," Constantine said.

"I hope you're right. Pulling off what you have in mind will take nothing short of a miracle."

27

Asiyah pressed her body tighter against his powerful back as Sokolov steered the scooter through a web of streets and alleys. The menacing sound of the preying chopper receded as they left Grunewald far behind. The massacre site at Palais Pannwitz would be crawling with *Bundespolizei* officers by now. They'd narrowly escaped the bloodbath and slipped away from the counter-terrorism unit, but still had nowhere to go, no place to hide.

"Do you know any decent nightclubs in this town?" Sokolov asked.

"Are you kidding? Berlin is the clubbing capital of the world. Of course I do!"

"Hard to imagine you indulging in that lifestyle."

"As the daughter of the Kazakhstani President, I've had my fair share of partying, believe me."

"Okay, I'm open to suggestions. Something exclusive and low-key."

"Well, there's this place called Blumenfeld. Very private. It's not famous, but you won't find a better chill-out spot. The atmosphere is unreal, in a good way, if you know what I mean. None of the crazy, drug-induced debauchery seen at other clubs."

"I'm not after the wild stuff, only a strict door policy against the *Polizei*."

"It's almost impossible to get into. But once you do, you could spend the rest of your life there."

"I'd rather not, but we'll see about that. What's the address?"

"Somewhere in Friedrichshain. The club took up a redeveloped socialist building of some sort," she explained.

Sokolov knew his way around Berlin, especially East Berlin, which the district of Freidrichshain had been part of. Their father taking him and Constantine on weekend trips to the capital made the highlights of his childhood memories. Twenty minutes later, he arrived at the club's location, hidden away in a former industrial area off Karl-Marx-Allee.

The urban landscape of Berlin may have changed since the reunification, but the communist legacy still reared its ugly head in the form of God-awful street names and lifeless architecture and planning.

The owners of Blumenfeld had done their best to mask it. The blocky edifice was bathed in a purple neon glow and covered with layers of graffiti.

A queue of about fifty people had formed outside the entrance. A team of bouncers let some clubbers in twos and threes, and denied entry to others, seemingly at random. The head bouncer had the build and all the charm of a bulldozer. A mountain of a man, well over two meters tall, sporting facial piercings in the shape of snake fangs jutting below his lower lip and a bull ring in his nose, which made him look even more formidable. As Sokolov parked the scooter and hung the helmet on the handlebar, he glimpsed the action at the front door. The bouncer was kicking a visitor who'd attempted to go ahead of the line. The young man, clad in a maxi skirt, crashed to the ground. Another tough-looking, mohawked bouncer dragged him to the end of the queue, where a couple of his beer-toting buddies picked him up and they departed, muttering obscenities.

"We're early," Asiyah noted. "The perfect time to get here is four a.m."

"We can't wait, and I'm not too keen on dealing with these creeps."

"I got this. Trust me."

Before Sokolov could say anything, Asiyah cut in front of the line and approached the hulking brute.

Sokolov followed her, calculating the most efficient way to dispatch the bouncer.

"Hey, Otto," Asiyah said.

The giant broke into a grin of recognition and replied, "Asiyah! Long time no see."

Then he eyed Sokolov suspiciously.

"He's with me," she said, winking.

The bouncer nodded approval, waving them inside Blumenfeld.

As they walked through the entrance, Sokolov could hardly contain his surprise.

"Otto?"

"He's a good friend," she said by means of explanation. "And so is Timo, the club's founder."

Otto slammed the door shut behind them.

They stepped into a tight corridor. It was pitch-black. A cacophony of electronic noise was blaring from the sound system. Although far from claustrophobic, Sokolov found the experience disturbing as he treaded in the darkness.

Then he heard a soft cry from Asiyah and the next thing he knew, he himself was in free fall.

A trapdoor had opened under their feet and they went sliding down a chute into the club proper, situated in the enormous basement.

Once they landed there, their senses were assaulted by pulsing light of every conceivable color.

As if in slow motion, hit by the flickering flashes, two or three hundred people were jerking spasmodically on the dance floor.

"Down the rabbit hole," she said as he helped Asiyah to her feet. "Come on, let's go."

Following her, Sokolov waded through a sea of humanity which throbbed to a thumping techno beat.

Crossing the underground floor, they reached a stairway which led back to ground level. Behind a row of doors were the club's darkrooms. A different kind of music played here, more like psychedelic trance. This part of Blumenfeld was cast in a muted red glow. Asiyah guided him into a vacant room, so dimly lit as to render the surroundings barely discernible. Sokolov sank onto a creaky sofa which was the only piece of furniture in an otherwise empty room, with no other doors or windows. He'd been to a strip club in the sleaziest neighborhood of Paris, but it couldn't match Blumenfeld for weirdness. The surreal use of space, lighting, and acoustics produced an almost hypnotic effect. Only now did he realize how exhausted he was, mentally and physically. After the stress of the last few hours and days, even a worn sofa provided comfort. He felt his muscles relax. The melodic wave reached a crest and swelled in another phase of build-up. The outside world didn't seem to exist. He was drifting toward a state of semi-consciousness. In the semi-darkness, Asiyah sat beside him on the sofa and before he knew it, her mouth found his. She began kissing him voraciously, her fingers caressing his face and then tugging at the buttons of his shirt.

The dopamine rush in his brain was exhilarating.

He snapped out of it, disengaging from her craving lips and pushing her away.

"No. Stop it, Asiyah."

She arched her eyebrows, unbelieving that he'd rejected her.

"But why? Isn't that what you wanted? I thought you were doing it all for me. I thought you loved me."

"I do my job because it makes me the man that I am. Love? You're too cold and calculating to know what it means."

"But I do love you. I only want to be with you. If only we could make it to Switzerland together, I've got enough money there to last us a lifetime."

"Don't expect to buy my loyalty just because you've sold yours to Frolov."

"I've done no such thing!"

"What were you doing at the hotel, then? How did you obtain the false passport in the name of Erzana Mulić?"

"I have no idea who that is," she said defiantly.

"More lies."

He extracted the laptop from his pouch, powered it on, and opened the image of her Serbian passport for proof.

"Where'd you get that from?" she demanded.

"I pried it from the dead hands of Colonel Lisovsky, the GRU officer who ran the whole operation."

Her face looked troubled. She was cornered and she knew it.

"All right. From now on I promise I'll only tell you the truth. Everything I know. No games. Ask me anything you want."

Sokolov replied, "I don't have to. It's all right here. The hard drive contains gigabytes of data. I wonder how many files mention your name? Anyway, it's up to the boys in Virginia or Maryland to dig out. Cold, hard facts on your Kremlin connection and your involvement in today's terrorist attack."

"You're working for the Americans now?" she exclaimed.

"Not *for* them. Not even alongside them. I'll just hand over the laptop and walk away. They'll carry on from here."

"You can't do this to me."

"Give me a reason not to."

"You *must* believe me, Eugene! I'm the deceived, not the deceiver!" She sobbed. "I was told to meet with Ivanov to discuss an offer. It was a set-up."

"Who's Ivanov? The man they abducted?"

"Dmitry Ivanov, Nobel Laureate in Physics."

"What do they want him for? Mercury-18?"

"You do know quite a lot."

"Only that it has something to do with weather manipulation, earthquakes, and Tesla."

"The short answer is yes."

"And the long answer?"

She sighed. "Even with my degree and all, I'm not sure if I can explain it to you."

"Try me."

"Okay. Well, Mercury-18 is based on Tesla's discovery of longitudinal scalar waves. By around 1960, Soviet scientists had weaponized his electromagnetic research, and they spent the next thirty years advancing it. The so-called Tesla howitzers are actually interferometers which operate by tapping into scalar EM waves. Hostile weather engineering is one of their earliest capabilities. The electromagnetic blasts can be used in either heating or cooling mode, thus altering the weather at any given target. Earthquakes, on the other hand, can be triggered by directing scalar energy at seismic fault lines. It's a lot more complex, so this stage of Mercury-18 stalled until the Soviet Union collapsed. But Dmitry Ivanov was the Mercury-18 project leader during the final testing phase—which he never had the chance to complete."

"So now he's been offered another opportunity. What if he turns it down?"

"In any case, Mercury-18's development will continue where it left off in 1991, which still presents a massive head start over the West. You see, behind the scenes Ivanov has been a staunch advocate of scalar weapons parity. He's lobbied for the creation of an EM defense system to balance out Moscow's advantage. His disappearance has virtually squashed any chance of the U.S. catching up with Russia any time soon."

"And coercing Ivanov to work for the Kremlin will end the new arms race before it even started," Sokolov surmised. "Do you know where they've taken him?"

"No. I don't. And I have no idea what their next step is. That's it. Make of that what you will," she concluded.

"Are you still going to turn me over to the Americans?"

He sighed. "Asiyah, there's no easy way out of this mess for you. My priority is getting out of Germany. You can stay here, or follow along, or run off to Switzerland or any other country from Austria to Zimbabwe. But you must realize that you'll get caught eventually, either by the Americans or the Russians. Are you ready to live the rest of your life as a fugitive? It's up to you. Right now, I'm just interested in survival."

"You're right, of course. There's only one side that's marked me for death, and it's not the U.S. I'd be willing to cooperate under their witness protection program. It has its perks. The CIA is nowhere near as bad as the SVR or—Allah forbid—the GRU, so I hope you can broker a deal."

"You have an entitled mindset, princess. With government agencies, you always get the worst end of the bargain. I don't make promises I can't keep. Let's see if we're still alive by this time tomorrow. Until then, we'll have to improvise."

There wasn't an awful lot he could do at all right now. He hated the futility, but he knew that if there was one person he could depend on, it was his brother. It might prove too big a challenge for Constantine, but they were short on options. He raked his memory for his father's old contacts he could turn to, but came up empty. Unless Constantine could figure out an escape plan, they were screwed. Time was running out. Sooner or later, the German authorities would zero in on him and Asiyah. And then only God knew what would happen next. The Germans didn't want any trouble, so a hush-hush extradition back to Russia seemed probable, right into the hands of the FSB and the cellars of the Lubyanka. He didn't completely trust Hilton, either. Their partnership had been pretty one-sided so far.

A notification popped up. Incoming message. From the moment he opened it, he knew they had a break-through.

As he read it, he felt a wave of renewed hope and said a silent prayer of thanks.

"What is it?" Asiyah asked.

"A lifeline. Someone's agreed to bail us out and take us to a safe house—in exchange for information. The rendezvous is a few blocks away from here. Are you on board?"

"The price seems reasonable. I'm in. How soon should we get going?"

"Now. There's no time to spare. Come on."

He crammed the laptop into the bag and started toward the exit.

"Nobody's leaving," boomed a deep male voice.

Outlined by the dim light, Otto's imposing shape filled the doorway as another man stormed into the darkroom ahead of him. The intruder boasted a trendy quiff haircut and a satin shirt, buttons undone to reveal a waxed chest.

"What nonsense. You want to party to the end," the man said. "Can I offer you some booze? Or maybe some coke?"

Sokolov could wager that he wasn't talking about the soda drink.

"Timo, my dear," Asiyah said, "you run the best club in Berlin, but we really must go."

His outstretched arm barred her path.

"I insist that you remain here as my guests. Or else you'll have to deal with Otto. The only thing he's better at than keeping people out of this place is keeping them in." Beneath the arrogant tone, there was menace in his voice.

"Too much hospitality can get annoying, even at your club."

His mouth twisted, baring his whitened teeth.

"I'm sorry, Asiyah. I'm so sorry. But you know that Blumenfeld wouldn't last long without rich Russian clients. One of them told me to be on the lookout for your pretty face. I'm simply returning a favor. I just got off the phone with a man from the Russian embassy who should arrive here any minute now. And afterwards ... what happens in Blumenfeld, stays in Blumenfeld."

Instantly, Asiyah slapped a stinging open-hand strike across Timo's face that snapped his head sideways. Bleeding red gashes appeared on his left cheek as if he'd been clawed by a tiger. Then Asiyah's rigid backhand chop to the throat cut off his miserable cry and sent him sprawling on the floor.

A split second before Otto could respond, Sokolov swiped at the bull piercing in his nose and ripped it out. As the brute clasped his blood-spewing snout in complete shock, Sokolov drove a fierce upside-down-fisted *ura-tsuki* punch into his solar plexus. The explosion of pain caused Otto to double over. Sokolov whacked the nape of his neck with an elbow, striking the cerebellum, and the behemoth bouncer toppled next to his boss.

Sokolov grabbed Asiyah's hand and together they ran out of the darkroom.

"There has to be another way out of this hellhole," he said. "I'm not climbing up that damned chute."

"The fire escape!"

They rushed through the door marked *Ausgang*. Out in the street, they were met by driving rain. They rounded the corner of the building, running toward the waiting Vespa.

Otto's mohawked henchman was standing next to it, keeping watch.

"Get away from my scooter!" Sokolov warned.

Instead of heeding his warning, the bouncer launched himself at Sokolov, throwing a wild punch.

The battle was short-lived. Sokolov dodged his attack and countered with a spinning backfist that battered the hood in the face, teeth flying. The bouncer hit the ground as if scythed, and stayed there. By the time his buddies showed up, the Vespa would be long gone.

The scooter charged through the nocturnal city. In the distance, the Berlin TV tower jutted out like a beacon guiding Sokolov to Alexanderplatz, making it easy to navigate to the neighboring locality of Prenzlauer Berg where their stopover lay. The Vespa would reach it within minutes. The journey to the CIA safe house itself would take far longer. He hadn't told Asiyah that the safe house—or rather, black site—was located somewhere in Poland.

28

German *Kanzlerin* Augusta Müller felt stabbing pain as if her head were being squeezed by a vise. She massaged her temples as she left her desk and approached the tall window overlooking the Reichstag and beyond, the Brandenburg Gate. Located on the bank of the River Spree, the postmodern Chancellery was a cubic structure of white concrete walls, glass, and irregular-shaped columns. On the top floor, eight levels above the 19,000 square meters of government headquarters, was a special apartment reserved for the Chancellor. She did not frequent the 200-square-meter flat, preferring the comfort of her private home to the utilitarian space taken up mostly by the two large briefing rooms, with only 28 square meters left for the unused lounge, kitchen, and south-facing bedroom. But tonight the occasion was far from normal. Augusta Müller was facing her biggest crisis as *Bundeskanzlerin*. And she was alone. She needed the kind of seclusion that only the *Kanzlerapartment* provided.

She'd just finished reading the urgent, top-secret BND brief on the killings at Palais Pannwitz. The palace had become a slaughterhouse.

Count de Grenier was dead. Harry Richardson, dead. Forty-four other dignitaries from around the world, brutally murdered.

The world would never learn about the heinous crime. It would have to remain as secret as the Brandenburg Club meeting itself.

There would be no day of mourning, no media coverage, no *#IchbinEinBerliner* hashtags on social media.

Even the Bundestag members would have to be kept in the dark. The very coalition which had backed her for another term as Chancellor, despite Russia's efforts to sow discord and meddle in the German parliamentary elections.

Already a plan was set into motion to cover up the sudden disappearance of the slain Brandenburg Club members. A heart attack. A suicide. A boating accident. Death by an assortment of other natural causes and tragic mishaps. Each announcement timed days or even weeks apart to arouse no suspicion.

And above all, the terrorists had to be hunted down and exterminated without public knowledge. As soon as possible, before they could carry out a follow-up attack.

No other world leader had been made aware of the Schlosshotel wipeout. Augusta Müller was about to phone the U.S. President and inform him when an unexpected call came through to her.

It was from the Kremlin, said the *Kanzleramt* operator. She answered it.

"Good evening, Frau Chancellor," said Russian President Saveliy Frolov. His adequate command of English eliminated the necessity of an interpreter.

"Good evening, Herr Frolov," said Müller coolly.

"Please accept my condolences in relation to tonight's despicable act of terror in Grunewald." Frolov's voice sounded raspy.

How could he possibly know? she thought desperately. It was inconceivable, unless . . .

During the reunification, West German intelligence had recovered the names of Stasi officers and agents working throughout East Germany.

But the vast network of Stasi agents operating in *West* Germany had never been unveiled. The secret documents containing their identities had been shipped to Moscow as the Berlin Wall had fallen.

Some of them could still be active, working in the top hierarchy of the BND. Perhaps a high-ranking mole had leaked the information to the Kremlin.

The alternative seemed even more frightening.

According to the BND, the terrorists killed in the hotel belonged to a radical organization called the Islamic Levant. Its origins, while not entirely clear, could be traced to the Russians. Its leadership consisted of Saddam Hussein's Soviet-trained generals who'd flocked from Iraq to Syria, under the protection of the Kremlin-propped regime. Also, the Levant largely recruited its fighters among Muslims in Russia and other ex-Soviet republics. Inciting conflict in the Middle East helped Russia increase the tide of refugees flooding into Europe. Perhaps among the thousands of migrants arriving each year to Germany were sleeper cells of GRU-controlled jihadis.

What were the odds of Frolov sanctioning the attack himself?

Deep down, the *Kanzlerin* could not rule it out.

"Herr Frolov, what is the purpose of your call?"

"A proposal."

"I'm listening."

"On behalf of the Russian Federation, I'd like to extend my full support to Germany as the leading EU country. We must put aside our differences and join forces to fight global terrorism. Russia has always been on the forefront of the war on terror. We are open to constructive dialog. Russia is ready to share vital intelligence with Europe. But we can only do it on equal terms."

"What are you trying to say? I don't understand."

"The humiliating sanctions against Russia must be lifted," Frolov demanded. "And we expect the same level of commitment to our partnership and exchange of intelligence data."

"We do stand united, Herr Frolov, I assure you. United with our American allies in making you follow international law."

"America!" Frolov spat. "Can't you see that it's the White House that is interfering with the affairs of other nations? Europe should stop following the U.S. blindly. The United States are the ones sponsoring the likes of the Islamic Levant. Russian intelligence services possess irrefutable proof, but you're refusing to consider it. The attack in Grunewald is the latest in a long list of American black flag operations."

"Is that so?" Augusta Müller was beginning to lose her temper. "In that case, there is one piece of intel that I can share with you. The BND has identified a suspect in the attack. He is a Russian officer, Eugene Sokolov. A survival specialist of some sort."

"Sokolov, you say? Ah, yes. We've known about him for a while. He's a loose cannon. Frau Müller, you must understand that this man is not acting in any official capacity. He has nothing to do with any branch of the Russian government. Eugene Sokolov has gone rogue because I sacked his boss. The FSB kept an eye on him before he left Russia—to carry out his deadly plan, as it turned out. I admit we made a mistake and let him slip through our fingers, but I hope your law enforcement agencies will deal with him appropriately."

"Rest assured. He is the target of a nationwide manhunt."

"Good. Very good. I'm revealing classified information, but take it as a gesture of good will. This terrorist, Sokolov, belongs to the same cell as Asiyah Kasymova, the daughter of the late Kazakhstani leader. She is a radical Islamist ousted from her country. Find her, and you will find Sokolov."

"Unlike Russia, the police here in Germany are capable of handling their job without my intervention, *danke*."

"Well, then. I've made the first step toward establishing cooperation. My offer stands. The ball, as the Americans say, is in your court."

"Herr Frolov, I shall not cooperate with you as long as

you wage war against your neighbors, abuse human rights, and undermine the democratic institutions of free nations. This conversation is over."

She could almost feel his rage flowing from the other end of the line.

"I can promise you one thing. You'll regret your decision," the Russian President said, "You will regret it dearly. Your countrymen won't know what hit them."

29

Simon Werner's fingers trembled slightly as he flicked the lighter. It wasn't the booze. He hadn't touched the stuff since breaking up with his *ex*-girlfriend a fortnight ago. It was the nerves. He was on the verge of the biggest break in his career as an investigative journalist.

Coils of cigarette smoke drifted to the ceiling of his rented two-bedroom flat in Prenzlauer Berg as he re-read the encrypted email on his phone screen. It was a tip-off from Magda Janowska, his Polish colleague. Like himself, she was an expert on Eastern European corruption. She was in on the scoop of the century, and she needed some outside help. Journalism was a collaborative profession, after all.

The story was so sensational that he could hardly believe it.

The Brandenburg Club, that elusive, almost mythical group of international power brokers, had gathered right there in Berlin to discuss the world's future. That alone was a bombshell, but it was only the beginning. Despite the meeting's complete secrecy, it had been subject of a daring terrorist attack. The top hierarchy of the Brandenburgers had been massacred. The attackers, posing as Islamic terrorists, were most likely Russian black-ops commandos. The German authorities were now covering up the whole mess, with the explicit knowledge of the Chancellor.

To top it off, a witnesses was willing to back up those claims and give a detailed account of the Brandenburg

Club's inner workings, the bloodbath at Palais Pannwitz, and the Kremlin conspiracy behind the attack. Allegedly, it centered around some sort of weather-control technology, which sounded like some crazy mumbo-jumbo, but Werner couldn't write anything off, yet. The source also possessed a classified laptop full of Russian secrets including covert operations in Europe.

If this scandal came to light, the shockwave would topple Augusta Müller's government.

Werner had told Magda right away that he wanted proper credit.

The facts required cross-checking, of course, but even if some of them were confirmed, they'd be in the running for a Pulitzer.

His part of the deal was source protection. He was supposed to provide a temporary hideout until Magda smuggled the source across the Polish border. That would take some doing, with possibly both the Germans and the Russians on their tail. Magda was a brave woman. Too brave, perhaps. Werner had long suspected that she had ties to Polish intelligence, *Agencja Wywiadu,* or even the CIA. It didn't really bother him. The notion of journalism as mere news reporting belonged to fairy tales. The former communist countries had a long history of recruiting spies among reporters, and old habits died hard. The CIA, too, had been known to use journalist operatives for clandestine assignments during the Cold War, usually to act as intermediaries in recruiting and handling assets.

Modern media were all about controlling the narrative. And the Kremlin excelled at it. The Russians had weaponized news, spending millions to spread fake stories through their propaganda channels. Even in Western countries, Werner had seen too many of his established peers sell out for Russian money, and it disgusted him. Werner viewed himself as an activist, fighting back against the Kremlin's lies and disinformation. The world needed to be shaken from its slumber for the war to be won, and Magda's story could be the wake-up call.

He considered his options. The risk was minimal if the story was a dud. If it turned out to be true, then his name would go down in the history of journalism. Heck, his name would go down in history, period.

I shouldn't get too carried away, he thought. A healthy dose of skepticism was a must in his job. Before he jumped in on the lead, he had to dispel any lingering doubt.

He took his Mini Countryman for a quick ride to Grunewald, five kilometers away. When he arrived there, he found the entire area sealed off by police cordons.

"A domestic incident," explained an armor-clad Polizei officer equipped with a submachinegun. "It's a precautionary measure. The suspect is on the loose, armed with a knife."

Werner didn't believe him for a second. Something far more serious was going on. So, at least that part of the story had checked out. There was no way in hell he was going to turn down a once-in-a-lifetime opportunity.

He launched the secure chat app and fired off a message to the username she'd mentioned. In a few seconds, the source replied in German to arrange a meet.

Sheets of rain lashed against the windshield as he drove back to Prenzlauer Berg, the wipers struggling with the increasing downpour. Prenzlauer Berg was a reborn bohemian neighborhood, combining Wilhelmine buildings, modern gastro-pubs, Soviet edifices, indie boutiques, and new apartment blocks like the one Werner lived in. Returning to his condominium, he eased the Mini into the underground parking lot and found a scooter occupying his allotted space.

"What the ...?"

As he got out of the car, two figures emerged from the shadows. A man and a woman.

The woman he recognized instantly. Asiyah Kasymova, the daughter of Kazakhstani tyrant Timur Kasymov, who'd run one of the most corrupt regimes found anywhere in the world. Tabloid photos didn't do her justice. In real life, she projected an exotic kind of female magnetism.

The man possessed intimidating physical presence. A bodyguard? No, a warrior. Werner had seen countless mugshots of Russian hardmen, conmen, and 'business' men, but this face didn't fit any category. His features had a refined ruggedness that suggested centuries of fine heritage. The eyes were alert to any danger and that icy blue gaze could made others feel weak in the knees. No matter what was going on around him, he was always in command.

"*Heißen Sie Simon?*"

The big guy's accent was impeccable, but with a hint of East German upbringing.

"*Ja.* And you are?"

"Sokolov. I'm the one you communicated with. And this fine lady here is with me."

"I didn't expect you to come here so fast. Follow me, please."

As they took the elevator, he noticed that their clothes and hair were wet from the rain. Reaching his floor, he guided them into his apartment. Asiyah eyed the interior with a bemused expression. The decor was a Nordic affair: white surfaces, clean lines, and practical furniture. Nothing fancy, but the space was bright and almost uncluttered. He'd bought a few vintage items from the Sunday flea market in Mauerpark, favored by young creatives and intellectuals, the area's prevailing under-45 demographic that Werner belonged to.

"Not the luxury you're accustomed to," he said.

"I've seen a lot worse," said Asiyah.

"It's a far cry from the splendor of Palais Pannwitz, though."

She tossed him an angry glance.

"If you want to ask me something, play it straight. Spare me this crap. I'm not in a mood for mind games, Herr Simon whatever."

"Werner. All right, relax. Here's what we'll do. We have a long night ahead of us. You're both soaked to the skin. I've got two en-suite bathrooms. Why don't you each take a nice hot shower while I fix some coffee?"

"Coffee?" Sokolov said. "Now you're talking."

30

Sokolov changed into the spare clothes from his backpack. The steamy shower had done little to soothe his sore muscles. His body hurt, reminding him of his old injuries. He felt the worst stabs of pain in his back, from the scars of Beslan. All of his fingers and toes were aching, broken years ago in the karate trial of One-Hundred-Man Kumite. His body acted as a barometer at times, and as he returned to the living/dining area, he saw why.

Werner had doused the lights, but the room was bright as day from the streaks of lightning outside. The dazzling flashes preceded booming rolls of thunder.

A violent wind shrieked like a banshee.

Then the hailstorm began.

Icy pellets bombarded the street, bouncing off the nineteenth-century cobblestone pavement.

The hail particles grew into tennis-ball-sized stones, hammering with increasing intensity. Like artillery shelling, the giant hail battered the cars parked in the street, crashing glass and denting metal loudly.

The roar was deafening. Sokolov shuddered.

Several vehicles collided in the middle of the road. Ruthlessly, the storm bruised buildings which had survived two world wars. People rushed inside cafés as the chairs and tables were swept off the sidewalks as if by a giant hand. The boutique storefronts were smashed to pieces and flooded. Visibility dropped to near zero as the power went out. The entire district plunged into darkness. The only illumination came every few seconds from the purple-forked thunderbolts exploding in the sky. Even then, Sokolov could hardly see the other side of the street.

Werner stepped closer to get a better look at the shocking spectacle, mouth agape.

"Stay away from the windows," Sokolov cautioned.

A moment later, another wind gust rattled the glass and it disintegrated into shards as a fusillade of hail cannoned inside. The coconut-sized projectiles bounced off the floor, bringing in a spray of rainwater that blew in through the pulverized window. A wind blast howled in the room.

"Close the shutters if you have any!" Sokolov commanded.

"All I have is the blinds!"

"Hurry!"

Werner darted to the manual handle and cranked it, rolling the window blinds down. The hail kept punching the coverings, which offered minimal protection and took a pummeling until the slats fell apart.

The rain poured on, flooding the street. The gale broke waves on the water surface. The ice bombs splashed into the water like torpedoes.

The gates of hell had shut as abruptly as they had erupted. The hail abated. The onslaught of wind and flood was waning. Sokolov checked his watch. The worst of the storm had lasted fifteen minutes. The severe damage that it had caused was immense. Sokolov stood mesmerized by what must have been the devastating work of a Tesla howitzer, blasting scalar waves from an unknown position. He picked up a hailstone off the floor. It weighed about a kilo. He dropped it in the kitchen sink.

"What next? Fire and brimstone?" Werner joked nervously.

"It's not the Apocalypse," Asiyah said as she entered the room. "At least, not yet. It's a distant cold explosion caused by weather engineering."

After a luxurious bath, she looked and smelled as fresh as a rose, even as the world seemed to be crashing down. Ripped jeans, white tee, black blazer. Simple yet elegant.

"Thanks for the outfit," she told Werner. "Are you sure your ex isn't coming back for the clothes?"

"I bought her entire wardrobe and she cheated on me, so I kicked her out. But even if she saw you like this, it would be the best form of revenge. The stuff looks better on you than it ever did on Sandra."

"Keeps me warm, too. It's a bit chilly in here," she said.

She was right. The temperature in the room had dropped by a few degrees.

"I guess this whole weather warfare thing isn't so bonkers, after all," Werner conceded. "Could you tell me more about it?"

They sat behind the dining table in Eames-style chairs—curved polypropylene on four pegs.

Asiyah recounted the recent events in relation to Mercury-18, the Kremlin, and the Brandenburg Club. Werner recorded the conversation over the next hour. Meanwhile, Sokolov checked the news feed on his laptop. Some cell towers were functioning on reserve power, although the weather conditions and the extra load resulted in a poor connection.

Scrolling through the timeline, he discovered that Prenzlauer Berg wasn't the hardest-hit locality in Berlin.

Numerous injuries and several fatalities were being reported across the capital.

The cost of the storm, classified as a supercell, was already estimated in excess of one billion Euros in damage to thousands of vehicles and buildings.

Winds up to 180 km/h had paralyzed the city's airports.

The flash floods and power cuts in the surrounding areas had disrupted train service as well as traffic along the main highways.

It appeared as though Berlin were under siege. Or a blockade.

When Asiyah and Werner concluded the interview, Sokolov announced the bad news.

"Looks like we'll be stuck at your place for a while, Simon. The city's locked down. No way in or out."

"Magda and your brother are due to fly out of Moscow in a few hours."

"The chaos will only get worse by the time they reach Poland."

"What are you suggesting?" Asiyah asked.

"I'm suggesting that we make good use of our spare time and try to figure out where the GRU is keeping Ivanov."

"It's like finding a needle in a haystack," Werner said. "Do we even have a haystack?"

Sokolov gestured at the laptop.

"Oh, but of course," said the German columnist. "And I have to back up all the data. Do you mind?"

"Be my guest."

Werner connected his phone to the laptop, mounting it as an external drive. As Sokolov transferred the laptop's contents, the copied filenames and directories flashed by under the progress bar.

"Hang on," Werner said.

"What is it?"

"A familiar name. *Rotfeuer.* Did you see it?"

"Redfire? What about it? Is it a codename?"

"A business entity. Rotfeuer GmbH was involved in a scandal which I covered. It's a shell company which, by means of several proxies, is owned by Avarus S.A., which, in turn, belonged to Robertas Dedura, a Russian oligarch."

"The man had close ties to Frolov. So how did one of his false fronts end up in hot water here?"

"Rotfeuer bought a large chunk of land in some God-forsaken area northeast of Berlin. They promised to develop it and create new jobs in a large-scale investment project.

Nothing ever came of it when it became known that Russian money was involved, supposedly channeled via offshore companies to circumvent the sanctions. When the scandal broke, the investors had a change of heart and everything froze before it got off the ground. Or so it seemed. There *was* some construction work going on, apparently, but it was carried out under tight security. Now the project is abandoned and the whole thing is largely forgotten. Strangely, Rotfeuer won't sell the land to anyone else, despite occasional interest."

"How large is the land plot?"

"Seventy-five hectares."

"Do you know if there was any structure built there previously?"

"Well, yes. The Soviets constructed quite a few of those. A Cold War era bunker is located there, but it must have been neglected for decades."

"There's your answer," Sokolov said.

"What do you mean? What could Rotfeuer have to do with GRU operation planned years in advance?"

"I'd wager this is where they're keeping Ivanov. It's their hideout."

"It certainly fits the criteria," Werner agreed. As the files finished copying, he clicked open several documents in the Rotfeuer folder. They contained maps of East Germany and detailed plans of a military installation. "Yes," Werner continued, "it must be the same site. Everything is falling into place now."

"A bunker is the safest place during a storm, isn't it. But there's only one way to find out," Sokolov said. "I must get there."

"Are you mad?" Asiyah said. "What if you're caught by the police? What if you get hit by another storm?"

"That's the whole point. Think about it. Right now, the police are too busy dealing with the storm's aftermath than hunting terrorists. Panin definitely coordinated his getaway with the Woodpecker attack, it's the perfect cover.

I must stop him *before* another storm hits. What if *this* hailstorm was just a warm-up before the main event? A blizzard or a hurricane. Whatever it may be, the next weather attack will wreak such havoc that we'll have no chance of escaping Berlin. Or it might kill us on the way to Poland. My brother and Magda may never be able to reach us, or if they do, we don't know what the next target is for a weather strike. I need to act before we're trapped for good."

"You're right," she said.

"And another thing. Don't forget, if this is the kind of technology they already have, I'd hate to think about the capability of Mercury-18 they will obtain with Ivanov's aid. I *must* rescue him."

"I'm coming with you," Asiyah said.

"No, I'm going in alone. This is as far as I've taken you. You'll be in relative safety here."

"That's not fair. You can't leave me here," she argued. "Panin must have a getaway procedure in place. If we bust Panin, we can use his pre-arranged escape route to flee from Germany."

"It's too dangerous. I can't risk your life. You need to get some sleep after what you've been through. Depending on how things pan out, I'll either come back for you in the morning, or you'll leave for Poland on your own. Make the most of your time until then. Rest your mind and body. You still have plenty to chat about with Simon."

Besides, there's no telling how Ivanov might react if he saw you again after you set him up, Sokolov didn't add.

"Okay, agreed," she conceded with a touch of bitterness. "No goodbye kisses?"

"No goodbyes," he said marching out the door. "I'll see you again. I promise."

"I thought you didn't make promises you couldn't keep."

31

Darkness swallowed Dmitry Ivanov.

It was the effect of the drug administered to him in the van. He had no idea in which direction they'd been driving him, or for how long.

He was hurled off the edge of consciousness into a deep psychedelic abyss. A kaleidoscope of horror images played out in an infinite loop. Time and again he saw the bloodied remains of the Brandenburgers. Like before, he tried to scream, but the sound was muted by the drug-induced numbness that he floated in. A yawing blackness enveloped him, and the last tokens of perception faded away.

Then, a thousand bright spots clashed and burst into a white flash. Ivanov felt blood rush to his head. A stimulant ejected into his system was forcefully accelerating his metabolism and reversing the artificial sleep. The first sensation that he experienced after the heavy sedative had worn off was a skull-splitting headache. It was as if someone had used his head as an anvil for a gigantic sledgehammer. He opened his eyes with a moan.

He could not focus his vision at first. Light and color were blurred in the eye-stabbing rays of a single overhead lamp, but as his mind cleared, Ivanov tried to make out his surroundings.

He found himself strapped to a chair in some cellar, lit by an overhead lamp. The nylon rope that kept him tied was digging into his flesh around his wrists and ankles. The chair was bolted to the floor, preventing it from falling over.

Two men wearing green fatigues crossed the length of the chamber and loomed above Ivanov. He identified them as the Schlosshotel attackers. Both had Kalashnikovs slung over their shoulders. Without their gas masks, he could see the faces of his kidnappers. Cold, savage stares. Twisted scowls. Heavy-set features. Thinning hair. The older of the two stroked his goatee as he studied Ivanov like a hunter eyeing his trophy.

"Who are you?" Ivanov croaked, his mouth dry.

"You may call me Panin," said the senior terrorist. "It's not my real name, anyway. Who am I? A Russian patriot. Unlike you."

Panin's boot lashed out in a kick that connected with Ivanov's cheekbone, the thick sole smashing into his face and opening a gruesome gash under the left eye. He sagged in the chair, a purple swelling already disfiguring his face. Panin hawked and spat a blob of slime on the Nobel Prize winner before getting on with the speech.

"You traitor! You thought you could hide from us in America? Wrong, you old scumbag. There's no safe place from the Motherland. Isn't that right, Umar?"

His jihadi-looking companion nodded.

"Mother Russia will get you anywhere."

To back up his words, Umar struck Ivanov on the mouth, splitting his lip.

Panin seemed to enjoy watching human suffering and hearing his own musings. "She can be merciful to her prodigal sons, though, and offer them a second chance. Consider yourself lucky that you can be useful to your country. You hear me, Ivanov?"

"How can you expect me to cooperate after such atrocious treatment?" Ivanov mumbled through the pain.

"Oh no, old man. I don't want your cooperation. I want your obedience. And I will keep breaking your body and your will until I get it. That's my job. The science part is best left to the pros back in Moscow. But if you try to trick them, you'll be dealing with me."

"This is insane!"

"Is it, really? I'm following the tried and true methods laid out by Comrade Beria. He was a great man, was Lavrenti. He built the bomb, with lots of scientists like you working for him, so his methods are valid. And our great President Frolov is building something bigger than the bomb. Something that will make the world fear and respect us."

Ivanov's blood wasn't only tricking down from his mouth onto his shirt. It was boiling. The anger somewhat numbed the intense throbbing that was shearing off half of his face.

"At my age I've got nothing to lose. I'd rather die than agree to serve Frolov. But I want to see you die first. We're still in Germany, aren't we? Sooner or later, the police will find you. They have to, after what you did at the hotel. They know I've been kidnapped. You're on borrowed time."

Panin laughed. "I have all the time in the world, you old fool. I can keep you here forever. This place is one hundred percent secure. We've got a direct data link to Moscow. You can work from here, for the rest of your life. Either that, or you will join Abrikosov in Kaliningrad. It's your choice. Nobody is looking for you. And nobody will find you. Everybody will forget about you quickly. As for me, I'm a small man. Unimportant compared to the pressing matters that the damned Nazis will have on their hands very soon. A series of storms, floods, tornadoes, you name it."

"You're a monster!"

"I see where your loyalty lies. Certainly not with Russia. Your lack of commitment to the country's cause is disappointing. We'll fix that. It'll take some work. Umar, carry on from here."

Umar approached his job meticulously.

World-renowned physicist Dmitry L. Ivanov was bleeding from multiple lacerations inflicted upon him by repeated blows to his head and face. It all felt so unreal, but Ivanov's sense of disbelief and detachment was dispelled each time he received another blow. The pain brought him back to reality that was more terrifying than any nightmare.

32

Sokolov rode the Vespa out of Berlin, maneuvering along the quieter streets in quick, short bursts. The autobahns were inaccessible, congested by continuous car crashes. Even the small alleys were flooded or filled with piles of hailstones and battered vehicles that Sokolov had to squeeze between. He witnessed the destruction brought upon the façades, windows, store signs, kiosks, and trees lining the streets. The city looked as though it had survived an air raid. Sirens wailed and ambulance lights flashed as the injured were taken off to hospitals. He resisted the urge to assist those in need. Berlin's emergency services were more than capable of handling the situation. The best way he could help—and nobody else but him could—was preventing the next attack. Besides, the territory he was wading through wasn't exactly friendly. He survived a few nerve-tingling moments as he passed *Polizei* vehicles, but remained unnoticed.

Finally breaking out of the capital, he hit a rural road which led nowhere but the dying eastern German countryside, the derelict, isolated villages abandoned for larger, more comfortable cities. Thirty kilometers away lay the large swathe of land owned by the shadowy Rotfeuer GmbH. He navigated by memory, the tiny headlight of the Vespa shining a path through the outback of the federal state of Brandenburg.

He turned off and continued down a dirt road. The Vespa's wheels spewed mud. He managed only a few hundred meters along the unpaved track when the scooter stopped suddenly, the front wheel jerking sharply. The Vespa got caught in the mud. Cursing under his breath, Sokolov checked his GPS coordinates. He wasn't far away. Instead of trying to pull the Vespa clear, he left the mud-stuck scooter and proceeded on foot. The soft, wet, cloggy soil squished under his sneakers. The light from the forsaken Vespa faded as he went farther. He stumbled upon a thicket and wormed his way through until he reached a clearing.

It was the edge of a hill. It had to overlook the vast estate of Rotfeuer, but the impregnable blackness made it impossible to know if this was the right place.

He pulled out his night-vision binoculars and zoomed in.

All he saw was an empty field surrounded by forest. Nothing to look at.

Then he gathered his bearings and adjusted the zoom.

Finally, he spotted it. A soaring barbed-wire fence that stretched in either direction.

From his position, he got a decent view of the enclosed area, enough to know that this was it.

The casual observer would still find nothing to see there. Or so it might seem.

Beyond the fence a road cut through the expanse of the privately-owned land. It led to a structure made of concrete, a large garage partially obscured by trees and undergrowth. A gravel pathway ran from the garage for a few hundred meters to another, much smaller building.

A wooden shed.

There was more than met the eye.

No ordinary shed came equipped with a blast-resistant steel door. The outward appearance—from the door's rust stains to the degrading wooden exterior—was deceptive.

It was a stronghold. An invisible one, though.

The shed served as the bunker entrance.

Concealed below was a subterranean fortress. Tens of thousands of tons of reinforced concrete, built twenty meters deep. Two-meter-thick walls and a four-meter-thick protective shield that comprised the ceiling. A ground area of 2,000 to 3,000 square meters. It would consist of a decontamination chamber, living quarters, an operations center, and a separate communications room for Stasi or KGB officers. Sokolov had a general idea of the layout from his NBC (Nuclear, Biological, Chemical) Defense training for EMERCOM, and the drills he remembered as a kid at the Soviet Air Force base in Magdeburg.

There had been 1,200 Cold War-era nuclear bunkers strewn around the former East Germany, most of them neglected now in distant forests. Not this one, which was rebuilt, improved, and fully operational. Confirmed by a couple of AK-toting sentries prowling the vicinity of the garage building. Most likely Islamic Levant or GRU grunts.

Once the enemy presence had been established, Sokolov continued scanning the landscape through the binoculars.

The gigantic area surrounding the bunker served mainly to camouflage its existence. But as he swept his gaze, he noticed something else encompassed within the premises, a few hundred meters away from fortified structure.

An antenna array. Rows upon rows of masts with dipole antennas mounted crosswise on top of each.

The original location of the bunker's tropospheric radio station was placed *under* the ground, not above it. Those arrays didn't belong to a communications network.

There must have been at least a hundred elements in the system. Sokolov knew exactly what it was.

The Cold War bunker hadn't merely become a terrorist hideout. It was a Woodpecker facility.

Sokolov marveled at the audacity of the Kremlin, setting up a weather-manipulation base right in the middle of Europe.

He put the binoculars away.

The lume of his dive watch glowed, showing the hands vividly. Pre-dawn, the ideal time to strike.

A mad idea, given the chance of success.

Without any plan or preparation, he was about to mount a bare-handed assault on a modernized military bunker capable of withstanding nuclear, biological, and chemical attacks. Alone against heavily-armed guards, total number unknown. He also had a vital hostage to rescue.

All of those factors suggested that he was foolish to even consider it.

He made the only possible decision, and nothing could sway it.

He was going in.

Life was not just a numbers game. In the end, it all came down to right and wrong, good and evil.

Sokolov was a rescuer. He'd faced impossible odds in his profession as an Extra-Risk Team leader. Attacking enemy strongholds wasn't his specialty, and he'd never done it before without support, but he'd give it his best shot.

He had no right to back down.

33

Every fortress had a weak spot, and an upgraded Soviet-era doomsday shelter was no exception.

The first line of defense he had to breach was the outer perimeter. The barbed-wire fencing acted mainly as a deterrent against wildlife and livestock, or accidental human trespassers. It hadn't been intended to fight off a determined invasion. None had been expected. The barrier was more of a part of the facility's camouflage. Erecting a tall metal fence would have immediately drawn attention and suspicion that something big was going on. Basic protection made the property of Rotfeuer GmbH appear like yet another area of farmland.

At three meters in height, penetrating it hardly presented an easy task, though. Far from it. Climbing over the fence carried the risk of getting caught in the barbed wire, possibly resulting in serious injuries. By Sokolov's calculations, the perimeter measured roughly six kilometers. An awfully long stretch of barbed wire to maintain. There had to be a chink somewhere.

He followed along the fence and soon enough found a section where the barbed wire wasn't strung tightly enough. There was the danger of motion sensors detecting his unauthorized entry, but he failed to see any placed around the fence posts. Again, the sheer size of the area that had to be covered played to his advantage. He took the chance that even if he tripped a sensor, it might be written off as another intrusion by a stray animal, not a one-man army.

He tugged at the loose wire, grabbing it between the barbs. He stretched it forcefully until the wire sagged, creating a gap large enough for his backpack to go through, which he threw into the grass on other side. Then he pulled himself through the opening, swinging one leg, then the other. He'd managed to clear the fence without ripping his clothes, skin, or crotch. Tackling fences and walls was an essential emergency service skill, and he'd really mastered the art.

No time for celebration. Sokolov focused on the next hurdle.

The garage.

The drab, concrete, barn-like structure presented a more vulnerable access point than the bunker itself.

A duo of sentries guarded the garage entrance, exchanging occasional small talk to combat the mind-numbing boredom. One of them was as thick as a wardrobe, muttering in a small voice. The smaller man, sporting a black beard, nodded profusely.

The steel door was unlocked, Sokolov saw, as it opened and light spilled from within. A third man emerged, wearing paint-stained coveralls. The big guy offered him a cigarette, and while they shared a smoke, the bearded guard departed. AK dangling, he rounded the corner to take a leak on the building's wall.

Now.

Sokolov dashed to the garage building, covering ground in a few seconds, and approached the weak-bladdered guard from behind as he unzipped his trousers.

Sokolov cut his bathroom break short, slamming his head against the wall. The guy's face met reinforced concrete with an uncompromising result. The only stain he left on the side of the building was a splotch of blood that trailed him down the wall as he slid to the ground.

Sokolov picked up the unconscious guard's AK, and checked the magazine, making sure it was full.

In the stillness of the night, his hearing picked out a foot stomp out a cigarette butt prematurely and the hinges creak as the coveralled worker returned inside the garage.

"Mahmoud? Mahmoud!" the smoking guard called out. "You taking a dump over there as well?" he said in Russian.

Not receiving a reply from his companion, the big oaf went to check what the hell was taking Mahmoud so long.

As soon as he appeared, Sokolov drove the stock of Mahmoud's rifle at the man's throat. Stunned by the impact, he clutched his neck, suffocating, unable to sound the alarm. The pain made him drop to his knees. Sokolov delivered a second strike to the base of his skull and he crumpled.

Sokolov picked up the magazine from the fallen AK for spare ammo.

He had a clear path to the garage now.

He burst through the metal door, ready to fire.

The only man inside was the worker, now donning a breathing mask and spraying paint. At the sight of Sokolov, he dropped his automotive spray gun and groped for a different kind of gun—his own AK-47, propped against his workbench, within arm's reach.

Sokolov pulled the trigger, adding another splash of color to the painter's coveralls. A dash of crimson blooming in the middle of his chest, a single round from the muzzle of Sokolov's weapon putting the finishing touch to his life.

Sokolov swept the lamp-lit garage for more targets, finding none. Something else captured his attention instead. He'd caught the guy literally in the middle of a paint job he was performing on a vehicle.

The DHL van.

The trademark mustard-yellow with stenciled red lettering had been sprayed halfway into a bog-standard, boring blue.

He checked out the back of the van, where Ivanov had last been seen. It was empty, save for a few wooden crates. Special delivery from Serbia, or what was left of it. The lid of one box had been broken open, revealing the contents. Frag grenades, packed like eggs in a carton. Sokolov grabbed a couple, stuffing them in his pockets.

He slammed the cargo doors shut and went to the front of the van. Up ahead, at the edge of the garage, like a chasm yawing in the floor, there was a steep driveway that descended to a subterranean level.

Sokolov snatched the car keys off the workbench and climbed behind the wheel, tossing his rucksack in the passenger seat. He kept the AK nestled in his lap.

The engine rumbled awake as he turned the ignition.

He thrust the automatic transmission into drive and put his foot through the accelerator.

Roaring, the van angled down the incline. He flicked the headlights on, going into the underground passageway.

The garage had its own bunker, Sokolov discovered.

It was a vehicle tube. A fortified, cavernous space where heavy military trucks could be hidden from nuclear fallout. Sokolov directed the van across it, to the next section beyond.

The forty-meter-long, cylindrical shelter opened into a tunnel.

The garage and the main bunker were interconnected, allowing protected access by car. This was how they'd brought Ivanov in, Sokolov realized.

The dimly lit tunnel ran 250 meters long in a straight line.

Sokolov accelerated and the van ate up the distance.

A concrete wall ended the tunnel. Its only feature in the middle of the wall was a colossal steel door, blast-resistant and gas-proof.

There was a remote control fob dangling from the car keyring. Sokolov reached for it and thumbed a button.

The motorized halves of the blast door whirred and began sliding apart.

Into the lion's den.

Or, rather, a large cargo loading area.

Sokolov cleared the threshold, parked the van in the middle of the platform, and jumped out, AK in hand.

He'd made it inside the main bunker.

This time, he failed to stay undetected. The area was under surveillance by a pair of wall-mounted cameras, their red eyes blinking ominously.

Sokolov had relied on stealth and speed. Now his advantage had halved. Only movement and reflexes could work in his favor. He rushed to the single exit—a narrow maze-like corridor.

And came face-to-face with another guard heading his way.

Sokolov was the first to react. At close range, a rapid trigger tap turned the opponent's face into a bloody mess, the shot booming in the tight quarters. Sokolov dodged the slumped corpse and continued, pulse racing.

Despite its gigantic area, the bunker was labyrinthine, broken up in a series of rooms and cubicles, connected by corridors, not unlike aboard a submarine.

The facility had received a makeover. The walls had been repaired and given a fresh coat of paint, and yet the decades of disuse had taken their toll. The smell of mold and decaying plywood hit his nostrils. Oddly enough, such Cold War relics as outdated maps of Europe and Soviet propaganda posters had kept their place on the industrial-green-colored walls. The bunker's electronic guts, however, had been ripped out and replaced with the latest equipment.

Security video cameras and infrared sensors dotted every corner.

From years of professional experience, Sokolov had learned that no matter how advanced the technology, or how complex the machinery, it was constantly beaten by one thing.

Human error.

His survival had thus far depended on it. And he had ample chance to test the human factor further.

He hugged the walls as he progressed through the maze. He didn't know which sub-segment he was in, but common sense and basic knowledge of the layout dictated that he had to navigate to the middle of the facility, where the operations center had to be located. He hadn't encountered overwhelming enemy forces yet. He'd expected the bunker to be teeming with terrorists. It struck him just how empty the facility was. In a way, he found it disturbing. Ivanov *had* to be here somewhere, and so did his kidnappers. Adrenaline pumped as he passed every corner, anticipating to engage the enemy.

It happened abruptly in the next moment, as he stumbled on a trio of AK-wielding jihadis.

Startled, they shouted and leveled their rifles at him. Bullets ricocheted off steel and concrete as he dropped back and pressed against the wall. Then he pulled the pin from the frag grenade and hooked his arm around the edge of the wall, hurling the grenade in the direction of the onrushing terrorists.

The grenade bounced off the floor. Panicked shouting sounded before it detonated in a reverberating blast. The walls shook. When the dust had settled, Sokolov heard agonized cries. He peered from around the corner to witness the results of the blast. Two terrorists killed by the fragments that sheared their flesh open. The third badly hit, lying on the floor, bleeding from his injuries.

Sokolov neared him.

"Don't ... shoot," the jihadi pleaded in Russian. He looked about twenty, still a kid.

Sokolov pointed the AK at the young man's face.

"I won't if you answer my questions. Lie to me and you're dead. What's your name?"

"Rasheed."

Calling a person by name was a powerful emotional tool. He needed every psychological trick for the human factor to work this time. A fine margin between life and death.

"How many guards left, Rasheed?"

"A five-man team. Coming here."

The young terrorist was responding well.

"Do they speak Russian?"

"Some do."

"Who else is here?"

"The boss and *his* boss. Questioning an old man."

"What's behind that door?" Sokolov enquired, pointing at the end of the corridor.

"Storage. It's empty."

"If you want to live, do exactly as you're told."

Rasheed nodded.

"*Das ist die Polizei!*" Sokolov bellowed, his voice echoing down the walkway. He continued in Russian: "You're surrounded! Drop your weapons and come out with your hands behind your head! Proceed into the room to the left and you will be spared!"

He yanked Rasheed to his feet, jamming the AK barrel into his ribs, and ordered him to translate.

Rasheed repeated the message in his native tongue. "Do as he says!" he cried in Russian as he finished.

The bluff would never work, Sokolov judged as seconds passed. It was never supposed to work.

But it did.

He heard the weapons clank as the terrorists threw them on the floor.

Sokolov kicked Rasheed, propelling him toward the airtight steel door.

"Open it!"

He complied, twisting the wheel handle that unfastened the locks and turning the massive door on its hinges.

Marching in a file, holding their hands up, disarmed, the five remaining guards entered the dark storage chamber.

Sokolov rushed forward and shoved his unwilling helper inside the storage room where he locked him up together with the five terrorist comrades, crashing the door shut, swinging the wheel to bolt the locks.

He'd done it.

Sokolov leaned against the door, breathing heavily.

He couldn't allow himself a moment's rest, however.

Now to take on the boss and the bigger boss. Umar and Vlad.

And rescue the old man.

34

In the video surveillance room, converted from the original news and information center, Umar gazed over a technician's shoulder at a bank of LCD screens displaying live feeds from around the bunker. He watched in shock as a lone intruder defeated his men.

"What the hell is going on?" Umar screamed.

The technician's mustached face turned ashen.

"Somebody's stolen the van from the garage, driven it down the tunnel and entered the bunker. Then he shot a guard, blew up a grenade, and then—"

"I know that, you imbecile! How did that happen?"

"I—I ..." the technician stammered. "I reported to you as soon as I detected the break-in. It was only a few minutes ago. You've seen the rest with your own eyes."

"What's all this racket?" Vlad Panin smirked as he entered.

"We're under attack," answered Umar.

"By whom? The *Polizei* scum?" Panin demanded with concern in his voice.

"No. It's him. Sokolov. He's *Shaitan* himself."

"The devil? What a joke. Send your men after him."

"I did. He killed half and captured the other."

"Captured?"

"They surrendered! We've lost all of our men, Vlad! How's that for a laugh, huh! He's taken them all out!"

"That's a shame. But it doesn't matter. The cowards had to be replaced soon, anyway. Spares us the hassle. Most of it, at least."

Panin raised his handgun and blew a hole through the technician's skull, blood and brain splattering all over the workstation.

"Useless moron."

During peacetime, the original Soviet bunker had been designed to be run by minimal staff.

Due to the top-secret nature of the Rotfeuer project, the upgraded bunker and the Woodpecker complex were completely automated. The weather-modification arrays were operated remotely from Moscow via the telecoms link. The place was manned only by a skeleton crew, a handful of Islamic Levant guards and the now-dead technician. A group of Russian military engineers traveled to Germany under false documents every two months for inspection and maintenance of the Woodpeckers. Otherwise, the facility required no human presence. This had sufficed—until now.

Suddenly Umar felt a stab of fear.

"He's headed this way, Vlad. He's come after the professor."

"It's the end of the road for Sokolov. And a new beginning for the professor. He looks broken. Time to bring the old man home. Is the chopper ready?"

"Affirmative."

"Good. I've radioed Torchilin. He's expecting my arrival. But first, we shall see this *Shaitan* off back to hell."

35

After a claustrophobic succession of hatches, landings, and chambers which housed the air cooling and ventilation equipment, reserve power supply, sanitation system, and assorted machinery, Sokolov entered a ten-meter-long passage.

Sokolov had to keep the momentum. Strike hard and fast. Keep them on the back foot.

A volley of automatic fire shot from the other end of the walkway.

Sokolov hit the floor and rolled for cover behind a thick pipework running vertically along the wall. The slugs zinged past and pinged off the concrete surfaces.

He had one more grenade he might have used to squash enemy resistance, but it was too dangerous. There was the possibility of Ivanov also being in the same room, and Sokolov couldn't risk killing the hostage.

Sokolov returned fire in short bursts. Emptying the magazine, he ejected it and inserted the spare.

The standoff continued as he shot a few more rounds. Then the AK fire from the other side ceased.

Having lost the initiative, Sokolov hesitated. He peered out, forced to make a split-second decision whether to charge forward in a surprise offensive or sit back and avoid catching a bullet if they were drawing him out.

Indecision in battle could be fatal. He went with his gut feeling. And it told him that something was wrong.

His gaze shifted to the ceiling, where the watchful eye of a security camera was monitoring his every move. They knew exactly where he was and what he was doing. They'd pinned him right where they wanted him.

He felt a chill run down the nape of his neck, and he pivoted not a moment too soon.

Sneaking up from behind, Umar attacked him with a knife.

A clamped mouth and a slit throat would have had him dead in seconds. Only his instinct had saved him from the Spetsnaz signature move. He evaded the knife thrust, ducking out of the way of Umar's swipe.

Sokolov swung his AK and held down the trigger at point-blank range, but Umar clawed at the gun, latching on and wrenching the barrel away from his body. One slug grazed his side, the rest missed as they struggled for possession of the weapon.

Sokolov yanked the AK, but the rifle was knocked from his grasp as Umar bodyslammed him. Sokolov's back crashed against the floor and the short, stocky Asian was onto him, driving the army knife downward. Sokolov blocked, arresting the tip of the blade before his face. Sokolov writhed, bucking his legs to throw Umar off himself and break free, but his opponent had him pinned down.

Behind him, he heard footsteps as Panin emerged from his cover. They had planned to counter-attack him in a pincer movement. Still a few meters away, Panin held off his shot. The two men wrestling on the floor were too close to each other for comfortable aim. But he was paces away from a sure kill. It might not be necessary, because Umar was winning.

Umar kept pushing the knife toward Sokolov's eye socket.

"Die, *Shaitan*! Die!" he panted.

His strength hadn't ebbed despite the red stain spreading over the side of his shirt. Gritting his teeth, wild-eyed, he was determined to carve Sokolov's face open.

Here and now, Sokolov's karate mastery proved irrelevant. It was no martial arts contest. Sokolov was locked in a primal fight for survival.

He felt the stench of Umar's body odor, vile breath—and blood. Life was sapping from Umar, but far too slowly to save Sokolov.

In a blazing-fast motion, Sokolov pulled one hand away, and thrust his index finger under Umar's ribs, deep within the gunshot wound. The entire finger dug into the flesh, which throbbed with hot, sticky gore. Sokolov clenched his hand, hooking his finger inside the wound like a talon, and tore at the flesh violently.

Umar screamed at the top of his lungs like an animal. The sudden, agonizing shock drove him mad, loosening the knife from his grip. Sokolov smacked it aside, and yanked his hand away from the wound, overcome with revulsion. He pushed Umar off and twisted out of his hold, reversing it as he spun around, sprang to his feet and grabbed Umar's throat, pulling him upright. Sokolov held him in a headlock choke. The man was practically senseless, barely standing on his feet while Sokolov used him as a shield facing Panin.

The tables had turned, and now Sokolov had a hostage.

"Where's Ivanov?" he shouted to Panin.

Panin stopped, lining up his crosshairs. He still couldn't get a shot off without hitting Umar, despite Sokolov being able to see the bead of perspiration on Panin's brow.

"Screw you!" Panin yelled—and squeezed the trigger.

Seeing that Umar was going to die anyway, Panin blasted away.

A bullet hit Umar in the chest, spraying blood.

Panin kept shooting. One of the slugs would inevitably hit Sokolov.

Flicking the pin away, Sokolov slipped the frag grenade into the pocket of Umar's camo pants, and pushed the dying man toward Panin.

Umar crashed into his commander, clinging onto Panin in a mortal embrace, throwing his aim off, the next shot hitting the ceiling.

Sokolov dived backward, clasping his hands over his ears as the grenade went off.

The explosion rocked the walkway.

The grenade had a kill zone of five meters. Sokolov had rolled just beyond that radius.

When he managed to get up, his ears were ringing but he saw that he'd fared much better than the GRU men.

Umar had most certainly been reduced to a corpse, his chest cavity pumped full of lead, a large chunk of his right thigh missing, the flesh charred where the grenade had detonated.

His GRU boss, alias Vlad Panin, real name unknown, lay flat on his back. Blood gurgled from his mouth and his stomach cavity, which had been ripped open. He groaned, propping himself up on his left elbow, blood dribbling down his goatee, his right arm shaking as he pointed the gun at Sokolov.

A final volley from the AK drilled his forehead and Panin's neck snapped back, his eyes staring lifelessly at the ceiling.

Sokolov dragged the rifle, staggering past the bodies. In spite of the horror, the fatigue, the disgust, he had reason to cheer. There was nothing more left in his tank, but he was alive, which meant that he'd won.

36

He found Ivanov in an empty cubicle in the living quarters, tied to a chair.

When the door opened, the old man started weeping.

"No more! Please! Stop! I beg you! I can't take it anymore!"

Tears ran down his face—or what had remained of it after a brutal beating.

Sokolov hadn't witnessed such a grisly sight in a long time.

The entire left side of the professor's head had swollen to the size of a grapefruit, caked with dried blood from several cuts, a nasty gash above his eyebrows, and a broken nose. Both eyes had been bruised black, and the left had shut completely. His lips were puffy.

"There, there," Sokolov said, comforting the old man as best as he could. "I'm here to help. I'll take you to a hospital. You're safe. Those scumbags who did this to you are dead."

"Is it true?"

"I made sure of it."

"You did the right thing. Thank you."

More than the soothing words, Ivanov required medical treatment.

Using Umar's knife, Sokolov severed the ropes that bound Ivanov's limbs.

The old man could barely walk, but Sokolov carefully led him to the eastern-most section of the bunker.

The last hurdle.

The East Germans had built helipads in the proximity of some of their bunkers, but during the refitting project, the Kremlin-funded Rotfeuer had gone one better. There was an *underground* helicopter hangar housed within the reinforced concrete structure.

Beyond the final door, Sokolov brought the elderly physicist to a jet-black Italian-manufactured chopper sitting in the middle of a platform. After he helped the professor climb inside the cabin, cradling him in a leather seat, he operated a wall-mounted switch, which engaged the roof mechanism. The ceiling parted, and simultaneously the platform ascended to ground level.

The helicopter was an AugustaWestland Koala, a VIP version of the popular AW119 model operated by law enforcement and emergency medical services across the world, from the NYPD to the South African Red Cross. It could carry six passengers and had a range just shy of 1,000 kilometers.

The distance to the Polish town of Szczecin measured under 150 kilometers.

In the early hour of dawn, the weather was the finest he could have hoped for, not a cloud in the clear sky. Nothing to suggest the previous night's terror which had shrouded Berlin.

Sokolov occupied the pilot's seat in the cockpit, powered up the single Pratt & Whitney engine, and took the bird to the sky, hoping that the terror would never return.

CODA

The chopper hopped across the border with ease. In under forty minutes, the countryside had nominally changed from German to Polish, but there was hardly any difference in the idyllic scenery. Sokolov pinpointed the location of the safe house—a two-storied wooden home situated in a picturesque Pomeranian setting of a lush green pasture by the pond, surrounded by forest. He landed the helicopter on a grassplot in front of the house.

Two burly Polish men approached the chopper and assisted Ivanov out, gently half-carrying him to the house. They were twins, Sokolov realized, later learning that their names were Marcin and Maciej.

The house had rustic decor, save for a set of leather sofas in the spacious living room. While the professor was being taken care of, Sokolov was ushered into a bedroom upstairs. Shutting the door behind him, one of the twins told him to leave his blood-soaked clothes on the floor, which he would subsequently collect and incinerate. Sokolov undressed.

After a refreshing shower in the en-suite bathroom, he changed into fresh underwear left for him on the bed and a plain black tee shirt and jeans. He lay on the mattress, closing his eyelids for a moment and opening them three hours later, according to the bedside clock. He'd thrown his Breitling wristwatch into the heap of discarded clothing, and it was gone now.

The sound of a car engine had awakened him. He dashed to the window, observing as a metallic-blue Toyota Corolla pulled up. Three persons exited the car. A balding, chubby man carrying a briefcase; a hot blonde; and his brother, Constantine.

He rushed downstairs and welcomed them at the front door. Constantine crushed him in a bear hug.

"Easy, I'm hurting all over!"

"You're an awful liar," Constantine said.

Constantine introduced him to Magda and the CIA guy, Hilton.

"Asiyah Kasymova is safe with Werner," Magda said. "Marcin is off to pick her up. He should bring her here tonight."

"Werner's one of the good guys," Hilton added. "I was mad at first with your brother, but his plan worked out well. Exposing the Kremlin plot in the media should yield a similar result to what the Brandenburg Club failed to achieve behind the scenes. Governments around the world will be pressured into imposing a new wave of sanctions against Moscow."

Sokolov told them about the Rotfeuer facility. "What about the Woodpecker arrays? They are still functional."

"I'll contact the German authorities immediately. The area will be sealed, and the weather-technology seized and neutralized. Perhaps the Germans will want to take the equipment apart and study it for reverse engineering. It might become a key part of *defense* against weather-control efforts, with Ivanov's help. How is he, by the way?"

"See for yourself."

The four of them went to the ground-floor bedroom to check on Ivanov. The door was ajar. A strong smell of antiseptic emanated from inside. Ivanov was lying in bed, dressed in pajamas, connected to an IV drip. Maciej, who acted as a nurse, had done a remarkable job attending his patient, cleaning the wounds and stitching him up. Despite his improved condition, Ivanov still needed a plastic surgeon to mend the damage to his face.

"Why did they do such a thing to him?" Magda asked, appalled by the old man's injuries.

Constantine said, "Korolev, the father of the Soviet space program, had his jaw broken by Beria's goons. It's an old NKVD tradition, resurrected in modern Russia. Remember the Great Seal story I told you before?"

"The U.S. Embassy bug?"

"That's the one. What I didn't mention is that it was created by Leon Theremin, a brilliant Russian scientist who invented one of the first electronic musical instruments and video interlacing, among other things. Upon his return to Soviet Russia from the United States in 1938, he was arrested, taken to Butyrka prison, and sent to work in a secret gulag laboratory where his captors exploited his genius for their nefarious needs."

"A fascinating historical figure, no doubt," Hilton said, "but I'm more interested in his modern-day counterpart."

He knocked on the door, asking permission to speak to Ivanov, who seemed lucid. Maciej let Hilton in.

He briefly introduced himself before asking, "Did they say anything while they did this to you?"

Ivanov cringed. "Idiots. Brutes. Degenerates. That's who they were. They said that I would join Abrikosov in Kaliningrad. The cretinous fools had no idea that I *knew* Alexei Abrikosov personally. He passed away years ago in Palo Alto, California."

"Any other names you might remember?"

"I'm not sure. Tornichev ... Torchilin ... Something or other. Not a name I'm familiar with. If he's a physicist, then he must be a lousy one."

Maciej glowered at Hilton. It was hardly the perfect time for a debriefing.

"Okay, that's enough for now. Have a nice rest, sir," Hilton said as he left and quietly closed the door, rejoining the others.

"Sounds like gibberish," the CIA man sighed.

"Maybe not," Magda said. "The name might not sound familiar to the professor, but it does to me. Come on, let me show you."

They proceeded to the living room and seating themselves around the sofas.

Magda took out her phone and tapped in a search string, nodding, content with her findings.

"Alexei Abrikosov isn't a person," she explained. "It's a ship. A research vessel based in Kaliningrad, currently cruising the Baltic Sea off the Polish coast, not far from here. At least, that's the official story. In reality, it's known to be a recon vessel of the Russian Navy. A spy ship."

"How do you know that?"

"I remember the Russian press release to deny the spying allegations, citing the ship's captain. Ah, here it is. His name is Torchilin."

"Are you certain about the ship's present location."

"Sure. There's a tracking app for civilian ships, you know, like a flight radar for aircraft. And the *Alexei Abrikosov* is masquerading as one. I got it right here."

Hilton whistled. "So that's how they arranged to smuggle Ivanov out. He'd be gone for good had they succeeded. We busted the whole scheme just in time, thanks to the Sokolov brothers. Good job, boys. Here's your reward. You've earned it."

He pushed the briefcase across the floor.

"What the heck is this?" Constantine inquired.

"Your pay. Two million dollars in cash. Untraceable hundred-dollar bills, delivered by diplomatic courier. And a job offer. Whether you take me up on it or not, the money is yours. A million each."

"What kind of offer?" Constantine asked.

"Research fellowship at the Harry Richardson Foundation. A Virginia-based think-thank that has a vacant Kremlinology position. We have to combat Frolov's hybrid war, Constantine. Fight fire with fire, and someone has to carry the torch. You're the best man for the job. Nobody has a better knowledge of what makes the Kremlin Khan tick compared to you. All expenses will be paid for by the Company, from your air fare, to your new home, to your wages. The Interpol charges against you will be dropped. A clean slate. You have no future in Russia, but you can help Russia to have a future," Hilton said emphatically. "But I want your decision right now."

"Well, I'd rather work for Uncle Sam than Uncle Ari. So it's a yes from me. What about my brother?"

Hilton hadn't expected the question. "Erm, hmmm, we'll think of something."

"Thanks but no thanks," said Eugene Sokolov.

"Gene, cut it out," Constantine muttered.

"Don't get me wrong. It's neither my ego nor false patriotism speaking. I have nothing against playing second fiddle to you if we move to the U.S. together. And I don't have anything to hold me back in Russia. But I can't do it, you see? I'd just feel out of place across the pond."

"It's better than feeling dead!" Constantine burst out. "You'd a wanted man in Russia now. The FSB will have your name on high alert. You'll be arrested or murdered. Frolov doesn't forgive or forget his enemies. You won't survive!"

"Don't worry about me. Russia is the largest country on Earth. No bigger place to hide. I'll think of something. Survival is my profession, after all."

"How are you even going to enter the country?"

"Oh, that's the easy part."

Constantine let out a defeated breath.

"Is there anything I can do to persuade you?"

Sokolov was adamant. "No. I've made up my mind. I guess it's goodbye."

"No goodbyes. I'll be dropping by to visit you more often than you think. It's only a nine-hour flight." Constantine smiled through the tears welling in his red eyes. Then Constantine handed him the briefcase.

"Now *you* cut it out."

"Take it. You need it more than I do. I'll be on the U.S. Government's payroll. You, on the other hand, have lost everything. It'll come in handy back in Russia."

"An extra million dollars usually does help." Reluctantly, he picked up the briefcase. "I'm only taking it because you're my elder brother."

"That's right, you listen to me and don't forget to write."

"I promise. I'd better hurry now, I have a ride to catch."

They hugged again. Eugene Sokolov swallowed the lump in his throat. Their bittersweet reunion had lasted mere minutes.

The sky over the Baltic was overcast, offering no warmth as the sun's rays penetrated the clouds, and the water was murky gray, like always. The sea was calm, however, and RV *Alexei Abrikosov*, a 108-meter-long ship capable of pushing 15 knots over a 8,000-mile range, was gliding steadily over the surface.

Igor Torchilin, the man wearing the captain's white shirt with gold-striped epaulets, was pacing the deck and squinting at the sky expectantly. Deep lines etched his weathered, silver-stubbled face, appearing much older than his fifty-three years.

The *Abrikosov*, equipped with a helipad, and two submersibles, was on a mission to chart the sea floor.

Utter bullshit, of course.

RV *Alexei Abrikosov* was a Project 22010-class intelligence ship built at the Yantar shipyard in Kaliningrad, from where the vessel was also currently deployed. The only kind of deep-water research that the *Abrikosov* had ever done involved hunting underwater fibreoptic cables to intercept U.S. intelligence data.

The present mission carried far more importance than ordinary espionage.

The fate of the Motherland might well depend on it, Torchilin knew. He'd been tasked with the exfiltration of a prized asset. Should he, Captain Igor Torchilin, succeed, Russia could obtain a cutting-edge military technology that would bring America and Europe to their knees. The grave responsibility put him under extra pressure, but also filled him with enormous pride.

At long last, a speck materialized in the sky. Growing larger until the shape of a black-painted helicopter and the buzz of its thrashing rotors were discernible.

The pilot expertly aligned the bird with the ship's speed. As soon as the deck team secured the haul-down cable lowered from the chopper, it touched down on the flight deck with inch-perfect precision.

The man who emerged from the cockpit, briefcase in hand, was wearing army fatigues and a balaclava concealing his face. Given the absolute secrecy of the assignment, hiding his identity from the ship's sixty-man crew was an understandable precaution, but it somehow irked Torchilin. The man was also quite a bit taller than the sea captain had imagined, having never met him before. What really unnerved him were the guy's azure-blue eyes that locked onto Torchilin's gaze with piercing intensity. He wasn't someone to be messed with, that much was clear.

"You're late," Torchilin growled.

"I know. I hit some bad weather on the way."

"Hah. Whatever you say. No matter. What about the scientist?"

"He couldn't make it. But I've got something better. Everything I need."

"The briefcase?"

The man nodded. "His research papers."

The captain sighed a breath of relief. He remembered the days of the Soviet Union's demise. Soon he would have his paypack, along with millions of his countrymen. America would perish.

"All right, then," said Torchilin. "That makes us ready to set course for St. Petersburg. Allow me to show you to your cabin, Vlad."

"Thank you, captain. By the way, I'd rather avoid using names, even fake ones. You may address me by my rank."

"Very well. And what might that be?"

"Major."

"Oh, really? Which unit? The Spetsnaz?"

"EMERCOM," replied the major, grinning under the balaclava.

Torchilin chuckled.

Yeah, those GRU bastards sure did have a weird sense of humor.

Made in the USA
Lexington, KY
06 December 2018